Raven H. Price

I0692267

Wisdom's Song

Raven H. Price

Wisdom's Song

Raven H. Price

DEDICATION

I dedicate this book to all women who believe in true love and romance. What would life be like if God hadn't created a loving environment for us all?

ACKNOWLEDGMENTS

I would like to acknowledge four people who helped me get this book published.

My husband, Ralph W. Price, III, who allows me to enjoy a writing career.

Joy Knighton, who beta read for me and gave me pointers and kept me going.

Shannon Baker, who edits for me.

Honorable mention: Michael Nesbitt, a dear childhood friend, (who passed away before the book was published) also read my work and gave me pointers.

Disclaimer/Copyright

Wisdom's Song

Artist: Ravenborn
Self Pub Book Covers

Print history
First edition published

ISBN-13   978-0692075418

ISBN-10   0692075410

ASIN:

Library of Congress Cataloguing-in-Publication Data

Table of Contents

Prelude

Here again, I've been appointed by God Himself, to interpret and narrate a love story of His making. As the Holy Spirit, I'm the only one who can filter His words from a loving viewpoint. Too many times, man misconstrued His intentions as wrathful. When writing the Bible, men took His words as disapproving instead of instructional and their views created flaws within the book known as Holy Scriptures. Now we are in the process of deconstructing some teachings to help people see God's loving guidance instead of having to live in enteral fear of Him.

Shortly after a confusing change in thinking, that was divinely orchestrated by God to change the way people thought about religion, I started teaching men the truth that God is good and not wrathful.

To make this teaching stick, Jesus made sure the enemy was out of the way. A set of events was designed to change a people's minds and didn't need Satan's interference. A complete disconnect between what was thought to be factual had to be explained. By removing Satan from this timeframe, Jesus made sure men could focus on proper thoughts instead of an evil whisper in their ears. Powerful angels had Satan in prison. The old goat was probably licking his wounds waiting for another chance to escape and ruin things for God and His kingdom, but it would not be today.

Sabbath rests were created for man, but Jesus never took a day off. He was always on alert, even in heaven. One day, He heard voices on earth that alarmed him. People were calling out to the universe for help instead of crying out to Him or God. He wondered if there were some demons left roaming around that were trying to take Satan's place and confuse God's children. Before jumping to the wrong ideas, he sought God for answers.

God knew Jesus wouldn't completely understand what He had just witnessed, so when He heard Jesus open the office doors, He shouted, "I'm glad you're here, Son. The Holy Spirit and I were about to send for you."

Jesus asked, "Is it about what I hear on earth? The people are crying out for the universe."

"Yes, it is! It's about time my family includes her in their needs and wants, don't you think? Zion is earth's source and the Mother of all creation, after all. She has been craving people's attention." God replied.

"Enlighten me, please," Jesus asked.

"Follow me to the observation room, Son," God said.

As God walked away, Jesus glared at me and transmitted a thought in my direction. *"Why the secrecy?"*

"No secret, Son," God laughed. "We can't keep secrets between us for any length of time. Before I show you something on earth, sit on my couch and allow me to refresh your memories. Have a seat and get comfortable."

We sat while God paced, "you are aware of the Eden incident that caused this disconnect between my thoughts and man's way of thinking. Adam didn't understand me after his disobedience and couldn't train his sons correctly. Instead of filtering my desires through love, he thought I was angry with him. When Cain and Abel were born, I loved them equally and gave them very important jobs to do. I told Adam that Eve's firstborn male would have to work the ground and plant the seeds I'd provide, so other created beings could eat. The second born had the responsibility of looking after animals that didn't need help from a man to reproduce. Adam told Cain his job would be hard because it was a curse, and this caused conflict between him and Abel.

Abel was grateful for a job, so he didn't feel left out of our plan, but Cain resented him because he didn't have to work hard or sweat to make something work.

I never planned for one man to feel less than another because of a Father's point of view. I love all my children equally. This division over who is more important in my eyes has created many forms of religion over the planet earth.

If each sect would take the time to find a common denominator through a loving viewpoint, instead of choosing what they wanted as gospel, then maybe there could be some form of peace for them to share on earth like it is for us here in heaven."

God stopped for a few minutes and glared into space. When he began to speak again, He quoted from one of man's Bibles. *"In the beginning, God created the heavens and the earth. The earth was formless and empty, and darkness covered the deep waters. And the Spirit of God was hovering over the surface of the waters. Then God said, "let there be light," and there was light"*.

After quoting the verse, He said, "I'm the reason man is confused. My story started off being written truthfully, but why I wanted it written down has never been divulged."

We still couldn't say anything, so God said, "I was lonely, boys! I needed something, someone, to share myself with, someone who didn't know me inside and out. That's why created a partner. Everything about her was shapely, her form was perfect, but she was wild and fitful. I had to help calm her emotions. When I realized she could not see or hear me, I created light. The brightness of it drove out her darkness and showed her my intent. I loved her. Through the revelation of my loving nature, a soul was formed within her being and she became the first of many to seek my love.

After we connected, on all planes, I named her Zion. My love for her knew no boundaries and it helped her return the same feelings. She allowed me to express my thoughts. Trusting that my love for her would never go away, gave her the ability to blossomed and she gave me everything I thought about. Things I'd only dreamed of, began to stand in our presence as a spiritual form. She birthed the keys to life into all shapes and forms. We were a family, and it was good. You see, Zion and I are the first husband and wife who became a Father and Mother.

Soon after creation was established, we created a man from dirt then placed the male spirit inside of his heart, so he could nurture everything we'd made. Nurture means to love and take care of, and it wasn't long before he craved a partner like I had. Rather than create another vessel to send the female spirit into, I placed Adam in a trance and took a seed from his spirit to make his partner compatible with all he was. Then we gave them a home. In Eden, they were to take from our love story and create their own kingdom. We provided everything they needed from the seeds of our firstborns then we placed the fruit in a tree and placed it in center of the garden. This tree was supposed to be like man's Bible. It was to be studied not eaten from.

Religion has destroyed any teaching about my love story. I couldn't bear this. Everything became about a wrathful Father. Zion had no place. I could not stand by and watch her worry over humankind. Her attention was designed for me only. Because of Adam's misinterpretations, the entire human race fought among themselves. You are our second male child, the only male left in heaven that was still a spirit and you knew how to love everything through your knowledge of me. I had no choice but to send you to earth. When I found Mary, a woman willing to become a surrogate mother for Zion, I wasted no time and used her body to create you a human vessel.

Jesus finally spoke, "This is why you are excited? You want more people to know how much you love Zion?"

"Yes!" God shouted. "She is my world, the love of my life!"

Jesus exclaimed, "Let's go to the observation platform, so you can show us your plan?"

In this observation room, God informs us, "we must start slowly. I've found two people who can benefit from Zion's wisdom and knowledge about me. The plan is to bring two cultures together who have been incorrectly taught by other men."

Then He motioned for me to move closer to them. Taking my hand in one of His and Jesus' in His other, He said, "I want the two of you, with Zion by your sides to repair a breach made from religion's twisted idea of brotherhood. Together, we will make a peace treaty by arranging a marriage between a Christian woman and an Indigenous man. For America's flesh to truly heal, this feud must end.

My instructions are for Zion and Spirit to influence Griffin Waters, who is an earth worshiper. Jesus, you, and Zion will be responsible for Odette Payne, the Christian. Once the two of them fall in love with each other and share beliefs, the science and truth denied them for so many years will reveal itself and their understanding of life will flourish!"

"You want more children, through them?" Jesus asked.

13

"Since time began, children who've taken on Godlike attributes, are all Zion and I have ever wanted. I want Zion's influence on our people to be a wonderful experience. I promised her that our kingdom would be a large one. I gave man centuries to comprehend why they were created. Being spiritual and earthly minded wouldn't allow love for others to flow.

Griffin and Odette's story will be an interesting one. They will learn how to communicate, and this will make shadows flee. Both will feel cherished. That's why I've assigned the Holy Spirit to interpret for me and keep their stories and thoughts straight. He knows how to tell a love story. He was around when I created mine. With Him, as my narrator, Griffin's, and Odette's tale, will go down in history without a flaw. Then I'll hear Zion sing again. I'll know for sure she is happy. It will be just like in the beginning when she and I formed a union based on love and trust."

"Why are you waiting for Zion to sing?" Jesus questioned.

"Because I will finally get to hear her nurturing our children instead of worrying about them and it will be music to my ears. Every word out of her mouth will be from Wisdom's point of view instead of a misunderstanding.

She's the only one who can tell our family how I saved her from darkness and the fear of loneliness. When she talks about me it will be music for my soul. There is nothing as sweet as a mother nurturing and teaching her kids to believe in a father's love instead of forcing them to fear him. I want recognition too. I love everything that came from Zion because they first came from me. True parenting takes two." God shared.

14

Griffin & Odette

After leaving God's observation room, Jesus, Zion, and I decided the best thing for us to do would be to study the two people God wanted us to marry. It was too soon to make face-to-face introductions or give guidance. We had to stay invisible until the times were right. We didn't know these two like God did. We had to hear their thoughts and watch their reactions to God's promptings before we could make specific plans to get the two of them together.

It was a Sunday when we started, both Griffin and Odette were not at work, so studying their thoughts and lifestyles wouldn't be difficult. To hear their thoughts, we had to pinpoint a brainwave and listen in on what was transpiring inside their heads. For other spiritual beings, finding a brainwave of thoughts would be like groping around in the dark to find a needle in a haystack, but not for us, we had the upper hand. Watching physical reactions would be easy. Thanks to Zion's creative ability, we would always have a light either from the sun or moon to see our way around.

Another thing in our favor was the time difference between Odette and Griffin. Odette lived on the East coast and Griffin lived in the Mid-west which gave us a three-hour difference to work out the details for the two.

When we found Odette, her thoughts were loud. Talking to herself was natural. Occasionally, she would speak to Jesus, just not allow Him to answer.

We followed her brainwaves while she was driving. Her thoughts were dark because she was complaining. An energy we associated with a spirit of fear. *"I don't like attending this church anymore, only old people show up. I don't fit. I wish the college church wasn't so far away. I enjoyed the younger crowd and the preacher wasn't some old geezer beating us over the head with a Bible. Paster Morris is sweet, but his hellfire and brimstone sermons don't enthuse me at all. If it wasn't for Mom and Dad guilt tripping me, I would be somewhere else worshipping."*

We watched Odette in Sunday School. All she did was fidget. When class was over, we followed her to the sanctuary where she sat with her Mom and Dad. When a visiting pastor walked in with Pastor Morris, we knew right away God was involved with today's service. This visiting preacher's topic was on marriage and family and it was bothering Odette.

She became very agitated and her thoughts began to scream. *Why hadn't I seen this before? This new pastor has managed to uncover a blinding truth. A very important fact about me! I was alone! Marriage has passed me by!*

Words have energy and this pastor's message was hitting her hard. Like lightning bolts from another dimension, her thoughts began to torture her body, hurting her head and breaking her heart. Her tortured thoughts took us down memory lane. The pain she was enduring while sitting in service was coming from somewhere deep inside her mind. We knew immediately her life's choices were to blame for the dilemma she was in with few friends and no life partner.

It wasn't easy listening to her mental complaints. They were negative and harmful, but only to her. She was thinking, *why had I been so hard on myself? Who was I trying to impress with a Doctorate Degree in American History? Who cares? No wonder people my age call me a stuck-up nerd. For years, my only desire was to feed on knowledge, learn as much as I could about America, then get a job, and find my own place and for what or who? At twenty-three I am already a tired old maid, bored with my teaching job and always unhappy.*

Odette swallowed hard, then faced reality, she hadn't dated, at all. Not even in high school. She'd spent so much time living in research that she hadn't researched a basic human need. Suddenly, she heard her biological clock ticking. Time for a family was running out. She needed a man! This thought was making her sick to her stomach. The only alternative Odette had was to ask God for help.

On the way home, she took her religion seriously. By faith, she really prayed to God and ask Him to send Jesus to save her. Her prayer was short and inquisitive. Was there a specific purpose for her? Why wasn't life correctly adding up for her? She was twenty-three and just had her first experience with a need to reproduce. She was dead serious, Jesus had to take the wheel of life from her and save her from herself.

While in her apartment, she continued to question her fate. she didn't want to be a virgin any longer. She needed to date but didn't know how to flirt. She'd never worn makeup or dressed provocatively to seek attention. Then, the thought occurred to her, *"maybe I was unattractive?"*

Curiosity forced her to run to her bedroom, so she could stand in front of a full-length mirror. She had to get a better look at what men would see, allowing her eyes to scrutinize everything from head to toe. She thought her hair was boring.

It was thick, a pretty shade of red, and wavy but she'd brushed it back into a ponytail instead of letting it flow around her face. Her face was blemish free but pale. That was fixable; she could smear it with liquid foundation and look tanned. Then she stared at her eyes. They were a pretty shade of light green and they would stand out with eyeshadow, liner, and mascara. Her nose was very feminine, and her mouth was sensual. She was proud of her lips and practiced throwing kisses at herself in the mirror. To her surprise, she thought she would be very attractive with a little help and wouldn't need plastic surgery to improve things.

Glancing down at her frame. She saw a slender body with all the appropriate curves. The clothes she chose to wear were frumpy and unappealing. After she dealt with the fear of being unattractive, she knew what she had to do. With a little money, she would look like someone a man would want to date. Hope returned to her soul and she felt a higher power changing her from the inside out.

Three hours behind Odette, while Jesus and Zion were helping her, I found Griffin. I would find out what God was orchestrating for him that afternoon before joining the others.

We knew God had placed similar thoughts in Griffin's brain just not what kind. We needed to know what angles to take to help him. Being off by one small detail would make things worse, for him not better.

Dark brainwaves were guiding me to Griffin. I followed him to a small home where he raged within himself. His angry thoughts were murderous. Not only were they killing him, they were destroying any relationship he could have with his Mother. I hated listening to his bluster as he stomped into the home. *"Why do I come here every weekend? Mom will never change. I'd rather be in a fist fight instead of hearing her berate me for being single every moment I'm seated at her table. I hate this fiasco! I hate this lifestyle!"*

"Hi, Mom!" He shouted.

"Come in, son," His Mom called back to him.

Keeping the conversation light, he said, "Ooo, something smells great! Are we expecting others to join us for dinner?

"No, just the two of us. I found an old recipe for duck and wild mushrooms. Your Grand Mother's use to cook them when I was growing up. I decided to make it for you." She answered him sweetly.

"Where'd you get the duck and mushrooms? Someone must have gone hunting for you?" He asked.

His Mom looked at him with sad eyes. He knew he'd opened the door for her complaints. Then she said, "I had to ask your Uncle Randy to go hunting for me and track down the mushrooms since my son has turned his back on our native ways."

"Mom!" He exclaimed. "I haven't abandoned our customs. I've been busy.creating the only Animal Hospital for miles. It takes up most of my time. I would have hunted for you if I had time. Things will change soon. I promise you! I'm looking for someone to help me run the business. I've placed advertisements at three veterinary colleges for a graduate student to train. It takes time for these things. Until then, I'm on call almost twenty-four seven."

"I know," she growled. "You even eat and sleep at the smelly place. I don't see a point in you having an apartment. You should move in here with me and save money."

"Mom, I'm a grown man! I need my own space!" He replied.

"Why? It's not like you are dating. Haven't you heard how the girls talk about you? Son, you are not only smart and have a business, you are handsome and, extremely well built. You remind me of your father. I understand why the girls talk and want to bear your children," she threw at him.

"Mom, please stop!" He begged. He didn't want to hear how his Dad made his Mom want to have children. Life isn't all about looks!

"You may wear your hair long and don a few pieces of native jewelry, but you're not acting like our ancestors. Most tribal men your age have a family already. I'm growing old. You will be twenty-five on your birthday. When are you going to make me happy? I want grandchildren to teach our traditions too before I die. It is imperative the Water's family line continues. The Great Mother didn't bless me with another child to carry on our line, so the burden falls on you," she threw at him, again.

There was no use trying to explain anything to her. Each time he did, his Mom wound up crying. It was hard for her to understand that he was not interested in the girls from their town or at the reservation, they only wanted to make babies and feel secure. They were pretty enough to look at, just not interesting to him.

Instead of continuing this conversation, he chose to talk again about her meal. "What herbs are flavoring the meat? I taste garlic but there is something different?

"It's wild thyme. Mother used it to enhance her poultry dishes. I'd forgotten she had some until I found her recipe box. Randy and I went to the old homestead and found where her herb garden had been. It saddened me to see all the herbs growing wild and unattended. So, I've transplanted many of her plants in my garden out back. The thyme makes the food taste good, don't you think?" She asked.

"It's a wonderful meal, Mom. I promise to bring you some wild game soon. It bothers me too that I'm not communing with Mother Nature like I should" He informed her.

"Maybe if you hadn't forgotten Her, you'd be married by now. Native men know better!" His Mom blurted, refusing to let the weekend topic die.

After they finished the meal, he helped clean the dishes then made an excuse to leave. Watching television inside his office was better he thought than listening to his Mom berate him and cry the rest of the evening.

As he drove to the office, he wondered if his Mom was right. Was he selfish not to want family life early? Lately, he preferred being with animals instead of anyone.

He liked sex, a lot. Women were beautiful creations, and he loved what their bodies offered him, but he wanted nothing more. When he needed a release, he would go to the big cities where he knew a few women with the same feelings. He certainly didn't want to be known as the boy toy of the neighborhood.

They Speak

We knew Odette needed encouragement, so she was given the urge to go shopping. Zion turned her attention towards Jesus and asked, "Can I be the one guiding Odette on this shopping trip?"

Jesus expressed to her, "That's God's plan. Just don't over-do it. She's not accustomed to spiritual voices yet. When the time is right, we can form a deeper relationship with her, our communication must develop correctly. Once she is secure in our relationship, she will interpret our meanings effectively. She needs both of us to teach her God's ways.

Zion clapped her hands in exuberance, then shouted loud enough for heaven to hear. "I'm so excited! I get to take my daughter shopping. Every mother's dream!"

I knew her excitement must be thrilling our Father.

This shopping trip was unusual for Odette. Sunday afternoons she liked to rest and watch television. If she had to, she would grade papers, she never went shopping for anything.

She made the decision to go to the mall and look at the clothes, and maybe buy a few items to jazz up her wardrobe. Since she was a school teacher, she always dressed conservatively, so most of the items she had were combinations of black, white, or grey. Those three colors always made it easy to mix and match her outfits. Even her jeans were black. It was time she focused on different colored items that would complement her hair and eyes and draw attention to her looks.

On the way to her favorite store, she heard a woman's voice whisper, "*look at those!*" She turned around to see who had spoken to her but, no one was near. Instead of searching for the lady, her eyes fell on some clothes in a small store window. The rich rust colors of the outfits were beautiful to her, and she couldn't wait to try some of them on.

She chose a long, gathered skirt in a bright russet that had a ruffled bottom to go with a silk blouse in black. Before she could get the blouse off the hanger, she heard the lady's voice, again, from behind her say, "*black will not flatter your face. Try on that green blouse hanging on the rack beside you.*" She noticed the blouse immediately and loved it, but where was this woman who's speaking to her? Not to raise attention, she softly asked, "Ma'am, where are you? I'd like to thank you for showing me these clothe and ask you for more advice." She heard nothing and tried to continue dressing without worrying if someone was spying on her.

After dressing in the pretty clothes, she gazed at herself in the dressing room mirror. The skirt and blouse were stunning and highlighted everything, even her curves. She completed the outfit by purchasing a short-waisted jacket that matched the skirt. On the way out of the store, she heard the woman's voice again. "*Accessories complete the look. Leather boots would be great.*" She looked around again, baffled. Then said, "who are you?" By this time, she was spooked that someone was playing a trick on her, so she left the mall and stopped by the grocery store to buy something quick to eat for dinner.

After gathering things to make a salad, with meat and cheese, she I meandered over to the makeup aisle. She wanted to see what they had to match the colors of her outfit. She didn't know what to buy. Most women wore eyeshadow, mascara, lipsticks, and blusher to make their features stand out. She knew dark brown would be her eyelash color, but she didn't know much past that. She reached for the grey colored eyeshadows but remembered what the woman's voice said about black tones not complimenting her face. So, she chose a selection of earth tones and matched them with a blusher in peach and a lip color in russet brown. A liquid foundation did not intrigue her. It felt sticky. Instead, she chose a beige powder to cover the shine on her nose. She didn't need color, just some sunshine to give her a tan. Happy with the selections she paid for the products and scurried home to try them on her face.

She unpacked the groceries and rushed to her bathroom with the makeup. Standing in front of a brightly lit mirror, she gently applied the eyeshadow, mascara, powder, and a light coat of blusher on her cheeks. She finished her artwork with lipstick and brushed her hair, so it would wave around her face and shoulders. She was a new creation! Then, out of nowhere, she heard the lady's voice say to her, *"you are lovely, but you still need accessories for the outfit."*

The voice frightened her badly, she worried the woman had followed her home? She ran to find her phone, so she could call the police. Then felt foolish when the room fell silent and still. She cried out to Jesus instead of dialing the police officers. "Lord, am I going mad? What's happening to me? Please don't leave me! I'm scared."

Jesus sighed, then spoke to Zion, "It's time, but I will need a few minutes alone with Odette if you're to have any success directing her. She has no understanding of you let alone ever talked to you. At least she's spoken to me. Once I've developed an actual relationship with her, then I will introduce you. Otherwise, we'll frighten her, and she will refuse both of us."

"I understand. Make me look good, please." Zion said sweetly.

Jesus decided to wait until Odette was asleep for His first visit. Speaking to her spirit, while she was in a dream state would soothe her nerves, help her relax and give her a sense of security. Enhancing her appetite would move things along quickly, so he made her stomach growl.

After Odette put her new things away, she realized she was hungry. The crisp salad items she'd purchased were calling her name. She loved the fresh vegetables, cheese, and grilled chicken combination. They always satisfied her hunger when she didn't feel like cooking.

After finishing the salad, she realized she was still hungry and went to the pantry to see what she had for dessert. She was thrilled to see she had oatmeal pies filled with thick creamy filling and grabbed two and poured a cold glass of milk to drink with the treats.

It wasn't long before her eyes grew heavy and she needed sleep. Since her tummy was full, and she was tired from all the walking done at the mall, she went to bed early.

Her dreams confused her at first. In them, she was running from the voice she heard at the mall, and this fear had her flaying in the bed. Her mind was in torment until her spirit cried out to Jesus, again, "Don't leave me alone! The Bible promises you won't leave me alone!"

Her dream changed instantly, a light hovered over her and she finally saw the face of her Savior. He spoke to her, "I'm with you, Odette. I've always been with you. What do you need?"

As if she'd known Him all her life, she calmed in His presence and managed to ask, "I need saving. Some woman is stalking me. and I don't know why."

Jesus took her hand and said softly, "There is nothing to fear, Odette. I'm proving to you I'm here and not allowing harmful things near you. I'm not an invisible force. I can manifest even in your dreams."

"I've never seen your face before. Why now? Do I have an enemy? I know I heard a woman's voice speaking to me at the mall then again in my bedroom. I'm scared." She confessed.

Jesus was looking over her shoulder. She noticed He was eying something or someone. Odette asked, "Who are you staring at?"

His answer alarmed her. "Odette, someone is waiting very patiently to meet you. At this moment, she is very sad. Tears are flowing down her cheeks because she wasn't aware of how terrified she'd made you feel. She will never harm you, she loves you dearly."

"What? Who is this person? Why does she love me?" Odette demanded.

Jesus shares, "Zion is the Mother of all creation, she is God's bride. Her loving spirit is the voice you heard. She is the voice of wisdom and wants nothing more than to guide you towards a fulfilled life."

Now, Odette was sad, Jesus' description of Zion was lovely. Odette said, "I've never heard of her. Why hadn't my pastor spoken of her? None of my Sunday School teachers have ever mentioned she existed. They always said to pray to you for guidance."

"I know, Odette. You are to pray for me, but not the way you were taught. Relationship means talking with each other. It isn't one-sided. I'm your friend, who will come running wherever you are. I'm proving that now. I'm here in your dream." He said.

"That doesn't answer my questions about Zion. Why hasn't anyone mentioned her?" She asked.

"Have you ever heard someone say, 'the Kingdom of Heaven or God's Kingdom?" Jesus asked her.

"Yes," she answered.

He expounded, "Anytime a preacher or teacher said those words, they were referring to her. She doesn't have one form. She can manifest into anything. That's why she is the Mother of all creations.".

"Can I see her?" Odette asked Him.

"Of course," He replied.

Immediately, the Mother of all creation was standing before Odette as a smiling woman. She was the most beautiful person Odette had ever seen, dressed in pure sunlight with a jeweled crown on her head full of gems brighter than the stars. Odette was awestruck.

"Hello, my child. I'm glad to finally meet you in person. Call me, Zion," she said.

While Odette was getting acquainted with Jesus and Zion, I was still on assignment observing Griffin. As the Holy Spirit, I would also have to be careful how I conversed with him. Fortunately, he had already fallen asleep after eating his mother's heavy Sunday lunch.

While he slept, I walked through his soul. Griffin's mind, will, and emotions were in agonizing torment. He was in desperate need of Jesus. Without accepting Jesus' spiritual connection to the Father, he would remain a very unhappy man. God's fatherly love is lacking for most earth worshipers. Not only did Griffin lack God's love, he had a problem accepting love, period.

The journey through Griffin's soul showed me many things concerning his history. Griffin's father had to work away from the reservation and wasn't home much. So, Griffin never experienced a deep family bond. He knew his parents loved each other because he heard their passionate sounds at night when they thought he was asleep.

He hated watching his father leave because he had to endure the company of his mother's brother, Randy, and his uncle wasn't a good influence. Randy drank most days. Griffin's dad didn't like Randy hanging around and complained about Randy's incompetence.

The family dynamics changed when Griffin's father died in a car crash and Griffin was forced to rely on his Uncle Randy for support. Which wasn't much. Griffin was twelve and too young to work and Randy beat him often for not taking care of his mother when he didn't. Native culture demanded a boy without a father provide for his mother. But in a continual drunken state, Randy couldn't teach Griffin how. Griffin had no choice but to rely on his brain. He purposely excelled in school and in the afternoons, he sought help from boys on the reservation to teach him cultural expectations. Everything became work for him. Even with the boys, playing and having fun was never allowed. If he didn't learn how to hunt, fish, and bring money in the house then he would get a severe beating from Randy. Hatred in Griffin's heart was strong.

When Griffin turned sixteen, he worked several odd jobs after school and on the weekends to provide money for the household. He also managed to keep his grades high. Learning was a pleasure that later paid off and awarded him a college scholarship. Being with his friends, gave him a love for nature and all animals, so he applied the scholarship towards veterinary medicine which took him away from Randy's painful torment.

He continued to work nights after classes and on the weekends, so he could send money back home. He never had time for the joy of a romantic relationship, even after he finished college. Guilt drove him to return to the reservation. With help from his friends, he invested some of their money into a much-needed Animal Hospital and worked hard to pay them back. Anytime his flesh required physical pleasure, he'd seek hurried and detached sex which was not God's interpretation of being loving.

Griffin needed us, but rather than manifest as a male representative, in his dream, I decided to take a cue from nature. Two animals came to my mind; a wolf and swan. Both animals required more than sex from a mate. I would use their lifestyles to prove to Griffin what he was missing.

I entered his dream as both creatures then began to speak with Griffin's spirit. My words, enlightened Griffin to something he already felt in his heart. I showed him the importance of having the right mate, someone who would love him for more than financial support and sex. He needed a woman who connects with him on a mental level first. I drove the point home by ending the dream dramatically. I allowed him to see the creatures mental and physical torment when a mate died. When Griffin woke up, he understood a necessary part of himself was missing and that was why he was unhappy.

Many Awakenings

Odette's alarm was scheduled to chime at 6:30 a.m. Monday morning. Jesus and Zion's plan were to prove to her they were not a dream. They wanted to greet her when she opened her eyes instead of hiding behind the veil God kept between the spirit realm and earth's reality.

The beep, beep, beep of the alarm clock annoyed her. She reached for it and turned the sound off then rolled over on her back to stretch. She felt a presence in the room without even opening her eyes. The hair on the back of her neck prickled as if she was in danger. She froze but managed to gather enough courage to slowly open one eye. She gasped at the sight standing at the bedside.

"Good morning, Odette!" Jesus said.to her. Beside Him, stood Zion, they weren't a dream.

"Good morning," she managed to squeak.

Zion said, "did we frighten you, dear? That was not our intention. We wanted to make sure you knew we were always near. You can always count on us being with you."

"Do the two of you talk with others like this?" She asked.

Jesus laughed and said, "If they truly desire a relationship with us, we will manifest in ways to prove we are near. Zion and I had such an enjoyable time after you invited us in your heart. We want our relationships to continue."

Odette tentatively asked, "are you planning to follow me around all day? I have to work, and I need to stay focused on my job instead of you."

They both laughed at her. Zion answered, "we are not stalkers like you perceived me to be. You can continue your daily routines without us in your face. If you wish to talk to either of us, all you must do is pray silently or converse within your spirit. We'll answer, even manifest if you need us too."

Not knowing what else to say or ask, Odette exclaimed, "good, because I have to go to the bathroom."

After taking care of her morning needs and rituals in the bathroom, she went back into the bedroom to find them gone. Her heart ached instantly, and she cried out, "Are you mad at me?"

We heard Zion's sweet chuckle again. Then she replied softly, "Never."

Odette returned to her daily routine; ate breakfast, drove to school, and dealt with inquiring minds. But, when she returned home, looked over the kid's assignments, she felt an extreme loneliness. The pain of being alone was unnerving to her and it brought back why she'd prayed for answers.

"Jesus, will you help me understand this loneliness? Why did I insist on being single until now?" She cried.

As promised, Jesus stood before her once again to answer any questions. He explained, "the loneliness you feel is temporary. God has plans for you, Odette. Remember your scriptural training. Your Bible says, *to God, one day is like a thousand years and a thousand years can be like a day.* Time is unimportant to my Father. Happiness is His idea. Trust His timing and allow us to guide you through the necessary paths that will involve having a partner. A man should find you. You shouldn't have to hunt a mate,"

Better than any teacher Odette ever sat and listened too, Jesus took the time to teach her things about scripture she never thought of before. He made her see a blatant truth, she needed to focus on Him more than the words in a book. He was her grounding and showed her that every chapter was written from a man's interpretation, even the stories of His life before the cross. As a teacher herself, Odette knew how perceptions of words could be confusing.

For the rest of the week, when she came home from school, finished grading the day's assignments and cleaning up after dinner, she rushed to occupy her mind with Jesus. He helped her to push away loneliness while they researched Bible history. Their time together made her see that her precious book was faulty. She studied the facts and saw where wars had been fought over what was considered 'scripture worthy.' King James didn't do people any favors by having a Bible written the way he wanted. His version confused believers and it has caused divisions rather than bring people together.

When Odette asked Jesus about her findings, He said all scripture pointed toward Him, but it didn't glorify His intentions properly. That's why He and God encouraged people to ask, seek and knock on their doors for answers when scriptures contradicted each other. Reasoning had to be explained by the Holy Spirit's interpretations. Love had to reign. Divisions were not their intent. His explanation made sense to her. He came to repair a breach not cause one.

On Sunday, Odette purposely did not go to church. Instead, she decided to pack a lunch and spend time outdoors in the sunshine conversing with the real Word and her new friend, Zion.

She had no clue where to go for the outing. She just knew it was a prompting from Zion to do something differently. She had the television turned on while packing her lunch into containers when she overheard a news broadcaster say an Indian Festival would be held at a local park all day. Anything involving history grabbed her attention, so she knew instantly this was the plan Zion had for her. She could do something she loved and interact with them in a way no one would notice. She was excited.

There was a long line of cars waiting to enter the park. This excited her instead of turning her away. Long lines always proved a good time awaited. She paid the entrance fee and followed the traffic to the picnic area. At first, she was disappointed when she couldn't find a table all to herself for lunch. Before she could mentally complain, Odette heard Zion say, "take the blanket you keep in the trunk and lay it on the ground close to the tribal dance arena. I'm sure you'll like being up close."

Odette loved her plan and didn't hesitate to gather her blanket from the trunk. Being able to enjoy her meal, listen to music and watch tribal dancers up close and personal would be great. Many others had the same idea, so she wouldn't look foolish sitting alone.

She was biting into an apple when a large Indian man exited a tent. She was not prepared for his beauty. Awe caused her throat to narrow and she almost choked on the apple she was chewing when he looked directly at her. She began to sweat.

Something was happening to her insides. No man had ever caused a lustful need to rush into her groin. When this man danced close to her, she had to fight an urge not to grab at his tanned, muscled flesh. He was a vision of perfection and she wanted him badly.

The beat of the music had her in a trance and the ground pulsed underneath her blanket causing her heart to join the rhythm. Odette's flesh was in trouble and she didn't know what to do. If she wanted to remain a lady, she had to find a way to tear her eyes away from this man and stop the pounding of her heart. She needed help and a moan escaped her mouth. She didn't have to pray for the Lord to help her, He understood the moan she made and both He and Zion showed up dressed in modern clothes and sat with her on the blanket. Their presence forced Odette's eyes on them instead of the most beautiful man she'd ever seen in her life. Having Jesus with her removed the grip lust had on her throat and it loosened her tongue, so she was able to talk. "Thank God, you came! What happened to me? I was under a spell."

Jesus said, "It wasn't a spell, Odette. What you felt was a body's natural desire for mating."

Panicked, she asked, "won't God be mad at me for having a blatant lust for flesh? If the man had continued to look in my direction, he would have known I was ripe for the taking. I don't want that kind of attention. I felt unclean."

He answered sweetly, "God is not mad at you. He understands the sexual craving for someone's body. I'm glad you realized lust wasn't what you wanted."

Zion leaned over and whispered in her ears, "I wanted to see if your mind could overrule your flesh. That's why I suggested you sit up close to the dance arena. I knew the man was beautiful and would get your attention. I wanted to remind you that sometimes, beauty is only skin deep. He didn't know you, but if you persisted he would use your body.

You don't have to worry, if you allow us, Jesus and I will help you. Right now, you need to breathe deeply and drink some of your water. Do this and your heartbeat will slow. and the refreshment will douse the sexual flames in your belly. When you are ready, we can investigate other things that peak your interest other than the man's body."

When Odette was sure her legs could carry her without shaking, she stood and gathered the blanket and lunch container. She didn't want a place close to the dance arena anymore, so she took the items back to her car. Jesus and Zion walked closely beside her. Their presence comforted her greatly.

They investigated many booths. Every owner had a story to tell. Only one problem. The story the natives told the crowd did not line up with Odette's knowledge of American History. Several times, she wanted to correct them but knew she'd cause a fuss.

The last booth they entered, showed pictures of the area where she lived. Creek Indians had also lived there. One picture, in particular, caught her attention. The tree in the picture was undeniable. The large oak tree was a historical treasure for their community. The people cherished its beauty. Odette could take anyone to its location. Beside the photograph, a sentence read, 'This tree marks the spot of the Creek Indian massacre.' This disturbed Odette. She could help but envision a bloodbath around this beautiful tree.

She tore her eyes away from the photograph and looked into Jesus' eyes, and said, "this isn't right. I was taught they left our area peacefully. I'm teaching the kids in my class that the

Creek Indians were given a better place to live and multiply. This sentence makes me angry."

She wanted Jesus to back her up, but looking into his eyes, they told her what she feared. She was wrong. Her college education was full of errors, just like her Bible. These Indigenous people had an entirely different view of what really happened.

There was no point in arguing with anyone at the Festival, so Odette asked Jesus if there was a reason they sent her there. He said, "God orders man's steps. He wanted you to see this. Zion and I will guide you correctly along the route and answer your questions."

"What route? How can I correct American History alone? I'll be a laughing stock for even trying." She exclaimed.

Zion whispered in her ear again, "the correction has to start somewhere. Let it begin with you. Why not follow the Creek's journey for yourself? Soften your heart and let history lessons of both cultures collide. Ask, seek, and knock and doors will be opened for you to understand the truth. No one should force you to teach lies."

Griffin's Undoing

It has been several weeks since I entered Griffin's dream as a wolf and swan. During this time out of his dreams, I watched him look and think about women differently. He realized not all women were needy, like his mother. He even hired Lucy Strom, an older woman from the reservation to help him around the office because billing and other paperwork were not why he went to Veterinary School.

Griffin was elbow deep in surgery when Lucy ran extremely upset into the operating room. When he asked her why she interrupted him, she said, "Randy found your mother unconscious this morning. He wants you to go to the Nation Medical Center. Paramedics have taken her there for treatment."

As quickly as he could, Griffin finished helping the animal and rushed to the hospital. Randy was drunk, as usual, when he found him in the waiting room and he couldn't answer any questions. Griffin went to the emergency room nurse's station and asked, "can you tell me anything about Irene Waters? I'm her son, Dr. Griffin Waters."

The nurse he'd spoken with asked him to take a seat in the waiting area and she would find out what she could. A few minutes later, a doctor followed the nurse into the waiting area and walked over to Griffin and extended a hand. "Dr. Waters, I am Dr. Arnold Preston. We think your mother has suffered a mild heart attack. She is very fortunate to have been found early. We plan to move her into the Cardiac Unit soon. As soon as she gets a bed, I'll send someone for you."

"Dr. Preston, will she be okay?" Griffin asked.

"She'll recover, but she must make some lifestyle changes" He replied with a hesitant smile.

39

Griffin thanked the doctor and went back to sit near his uncle. Randy was a mess. He smelled like he hadn't washed in weeks and when he talked his breath reeked of alcohol. Griffin couldn't hold down his discuss. He spat, "I'm calling you a cab. You have no business driving anywhere, and you can't stay here. You need to bath. Try sobering up before visiting mom."

"What about my truck? How will I get back to the hospital?" Randy slurred.

"We'll worry about that later. Just take your stinking body outside and wait for your cab." Griffin demanded.

After Randy stumbled off, Griffin called Lucy, so she could stop worrying about her friend. Then he sat alone while struggling with the guilt and shame of not being there for his mother when she needed him the most.

Two hours later a nurse ushered Griffin into his mother's room. She was awake and reached out to him when he entered. Griffin ran to her side, "Mom, I'm sorry I wasn't there this morning. If I was living at home, you may not have had this attack."

"It's not your fault, son. I've been doing stupid things." She shared.

"What?" Griffin asked.

Embarrassed she said, "I've been using peyote a lot. I also smoke marijuana when I can buy it."

"Why?" Griffin demanded.

"I thought they were better for me than taking painkillers. My joints hurt, and I can't rest without help." She confessed.

"So, you're a drug addict!" He insisted.

"No! I don't crave the drugs." She answered.

"I could have suggested things for your joints, that wouldn't have given you hallucinations. I'd even pay for you to have massage therapy, so you could rest better. Please don't seek Indian remedies anymore," Griffin said.

"I don't want your pity, Griffin. I do need your understanding, though." She said.

"Where are you buying the peyote and marijuana?" He asked.

Gnawing on her lip, she said, "remember Grandmother's herb garden? I found peyote there. It was almost dead, so I dug it up and transplanted it into my greenhouse. Randy finds me the marijuana when I want some. It soothes me more than the peyote, but I can't afford to have it around much."

"That explains why you've gained weight recently. Marijuana gives you a ravenous appetite," Griffin snickered.

"Yes, I do crave chips and ice cream a lot more because of it, she confessed. I keep stocked up on both of them."

To change the subject, Griffin's mom asked, "Will you do me a favor? I was paying bills when I fainted. They need to be mailed as soon as possible."

"Of course, I will mail them. Where are they?" Griffin asked.

"I placed them on top of your father's desk. I also need some clean underwear. I will not wear these hospital gowns without them," she said.

Griffin waited around a little longer to talk with Dr. Preston before leaving his mother's room. Assured his mother would not relapse, he left to fetch her undergarments and grab the bills for mailing.

He hated rummaging through her underwear drawer, but he managed to find the garments she requested and put them in a plastic bag. He hadn't been near his father's desk since his death thirteen years ago. When he couldn't find the bills stacked on the desktop, Griffin looked on the floor and found them strewn underneath the desk. Not only did he find the envelopes his mother had ready for mailing, he found a large alphabetical file folder that was held together by rubber bands. He pulled the folder out of its hiding place and wiped off the dust. For the looks of it, it was evident his mother didn't know it existed.

The bands broke when Griffin touched them, and the folder popped open. Before his eyes were legal papers that belonged to his father. One form caught his attention. It was notification of stock ownership. Edwin Waters owned stocks in Acme Engineering, where he worked and with Advantage Controls, Georgia Pacific, Griffin Food Company, Love Bottling Company as well as many others.

Griffin could not believe his eyes, so he sought out someone to call from the forms. He found Nathan Amos, a stockbroker in Muscogee, Oklahoma, listed on the notification. With shaking hands, he called the number on the phone and asked for Mr. Amos. When Mr. Amos answered, Griffin, told him who he was and asked if he had time to talk with him in person. At four-thirty that afternoon, Griffin was in Mr. Amos' office. He'd driven an hour to talk with this man and rehearsed the questions he had for him, but when he had Mr. Amos' attention, necessary questions failed him. All Griffin managed to ask was if the stocks still belonged to his family.

Mr. Amos requested Griffin show him a picture ID before doing research on a computer to answer any questions. When Mrs. Amos' eyes grew wide, Griffin knew he'd found the answers. Turning the computer monitor in Griffin's direction, Mr. Amos informed him that he and his mother, Irene Waters, were extremely wealthy people.. Edwin Waters owned stock in many companies and all the profits were being held for his family.

Griffin thanked Mr. Amos and informed him that he would be back with his mother as soon as she was better. Then for another hour, he fumed and fought an anger that tortured his mind. *Had his mother known about the stocks?* He wondered.

He hoped she didn't know. It was breaking his heart to think she allowed him to be beaten and forced to work by his Uncle Randy when they already had all they needed. He planned to get answers from her as soon as he returned to the hospital. The truth would be revealed without asking a question. He planned to watch his mother's face when he gave her the underwear she requested along with the old folder full of stock notifications. If she lowered her eyes, he would grab the folder and leave before making a scene, but if her eyes showed confusion then he could stop fretting and force his heart to stop aching.

Randy was in her room when Griffin entered, but his presence didn't stop him from thrusting the items at his mother. She looked at the old folder with confusion on her face. "What is this old thing?" She asked.

Joy flooded Griffin's heart. She didn't know about the stocks or what her husband had done for the family prior to his death. But the look on Randy's face spoke volumes to Griffin. Randy's face was red with rage.

43

"Where did you find that folder?" He shouted at Griffin.

"Why do you want to know, Randy?" Griffin spat back.

Irene pleaded, "What's going on?"

"Look inside the folder, Mom and read some of the papers. Apparently, Randy didn't want us to have what Dad wanted to give us. I found this old folder stuck underneath dad's desk when I looked for the bills you'd written out."

Irene studied a few of the papers and asked, "what does all this mean?"

Griffin answered, "I've been in Muscogee. I talked with the stockbroker who helped dad with these stocks. He informed me that you and I are very wealthy people because of Dad's thoughtfulness."

Irene focused her attention on Randy. "You knew about this? Why did you hide this from me? Griffin and I suffered because of you. What possessed you?"

"The boy had to learn native ways. His father relied on outsiders for support. That's not for us," Randy explained.

Irene orders, "Randy leave my room! I'm getting upset and can't risk another setback. When I'm better you and I will get to the bottom of all of this."

Griffin had listened to their conversation and had a new respect for his mother. She wasn't as weak-minded has he thought.

Preparing for Unfamiliar Paths

Odette spent the next two months, re-learning Creek Indian history. Instead of completely trusting what she read, she remembered to ask Jesus for answers, so she wouldn't misunderstand this journey He and Zion wanted her to take. As she studied, she noted certain routes the Indians made that eventually stationed them in Oklahoma and she planned to follow in those footsteps during her summer break from school to get a better idea of what really happened.

Odette lived frugally and had managed to save a lot of money from her paychecks. She would need most of the funds to take the route towards Griffin.

Griffin's new path would be wrapping his mind around being wealthy. Even though he was a Veterinarian, he didn't live richly. He was obligated to give half of what he earned to his mother, pay installments on loans to the friends who helped him set up the Animal Clinic, and then managed to live humbly on what was left.

After he and his mother claimed rights to the stocks they needed help. They hired a financial planner who showed them how to live without touching Edwin's original investment stock allowing it to continually reproduce. Griffin wouldn't need to work anymore if he didn't want to. The money flow created by his dad could sustain his mother and himself financially for as long as they lived if used wisely. Not worrying over and having to work to create a financial stream was something new for Griffin. For the first time in his life, he would be free from a heavy and huge burden.

On the first day of Odette's summer break, she decided to visit the old oak tree that grabbed her attention about Creek history. She sat on a bench stationed under the beautiful old tree, out of the sun while pondering the day's events. Not far from the tree, she could hear the Flint River flowing and closed her eyes and pretended to be back in time with the Indians who lived there.

While her eyes were closed, Zion whispered to her, "come to the river and let me show you it's beauty. Look for treasure there."

Odette did as she was instructed and walked closely along the river's edge. The rushing water was indeed beautiful. It was clear, fast-moving, and had minnows and small fish swimming in it with little effort. She walked for about a half mile along the water's edge until she reached someone's private property. Before she turned around, something caught her eye. An object was buried in the mud under a protruding tree root. *Would this be the treasure Zion mentioned*, she thought? With no one around to save her from drowning, she studied the water's depth before stepping into the river. Seeing that the water was only about two feet deep, she looked around for a long stick to dig with then took off her running shoes and jumped in the water.

She stirred the water too much with her digging stick to see what she had found and had to wait for the silt and dirt to settle. When something broke free from the mud and tree root's grasp, Odette knew she had a treasure. She reached into the water and pulled out a bowl made of stone. She tossed it on the riverbank and proceeded to climb out of the water when Zion's voice whispered again within the water, "dig further, Odette. There are more items to find."

Obeying her voice, Odette dug for several more minutes and found various stone utensils, evidence that cooking had taken place in this spot alongside the water's edge. She wanted to dig more until a venomous snake slide in the water near her. That's when she remembered she was on private property and must leave. She scurried out of the water onto the riverbank, plunged her feet into her shoes, gathered the items and ran back to her car. It was dark by the time she got home. The day's journey had moved swiftly, and she hadn't even noticed. She'd spent almost ten hours visiting the Flint River and digging for treasures and wasn't even sunburned thanks to the shade provided by the trees thick branches. She was only tired from the exertion. This also gave her a clue to the hard work native Americans endured to survive. Getting to eat was a chore. All she had to do was microwave a frozen dinner.

She showered and pulled on pajamas before eating. While she ate, she had the found treasures soaking in soapy water and planned to clean them when she was through with her meal.

The items fascinated her. They were of historical value and should be in a museum. Her intention was to take them to her college professor and ask what museum to take them when she unmistakably heard Zion shout, "no, you won't! Those items belong to you and your family!"

Odette had no clue why they would be valuable to her parents, but she didn't question her authority and wrapped them in some newspaper and placed them in a box under her bed for safekeeping.

She was very tired and needed rest before the next journey. Tomorrow she planned to drive to Mobile, Alabama and visit another historical Creek settlement, then to New Orleans where they followed the Mississippi River north towards Oklahoma.

Odette spent two days in both cities then drove without stopping along the Mississippi route until it ventured west to Oklahoma. She was one week into the route that Jesus and Zion directed her to take when she arrived in Muscogee, Oklahoma, to research and experience some of the Creek stomping grounds.

Griffin felt like Mother Earth was smiling on him. Soon after he obtained money enough to pay off the investors, two very capable Veterinary graduates showed up to work with him at the Animal Clinic. That when he thought it was the time to return to his native roots and spend time with his holy provider. Since he owned the business, had great assistants who could take care of the animals and had Lucy to keep everything else straight his desire to keep the promise he made to his mother grew.

Griffin drove to his mom's house to inform her that he would be taking a vacation when he noticed Randy's truck in her yard. They hadn't spoken much since he found out about Randy's trickery, and it gave Griffin a bad feeling before entering the house. He worried Randy would be drunk and giving his mom a hard time over her new lifestyle.

His worries were correct. Randy was huffing and puffing over his mom taking too many doctor prescribed drugs and having central heat and air placed in her house. In his drunken state, Randy claimed Griffin was forcing her to turn 'too white.' Randy had her very upset, and Griffin wasn't going to allow Randy's rants to make her sick again. He couldn't control his temper and grabbed Randy by the hair forcing him outside.

"Your problem is with ME!" Griffin shouted at him.

Randy's horrified expression said everything. He was a coward and didn't want to face Griffin.

"If you want a fight, I'm ready. Leave Mom out of it. I'm the one who had central heat and air added to her house. I paid for it, so she could be comfortable for once in her life without having to chop wood for a fire or sweat during the summer. Can't you see I want her to live without discomfort?" Griffin screamed.

Randy didn't say a word to rebuff him. He just hopped in his truck and drove away.

Irene was crying when Griffin went back into the house. It wasn't because of what Randy had said to her, but because Griffin was so angry. Seeing her that upset made Griffin feel like a heel. He quickly apologized and said he would go away, but she didn't want him to leave and asked him to stay for dinner. One day Griffin hoped she could see why he wasn't standing for Randy's abuse anymore; they didn't have too.

After Griffin and his Mom had a nice dinner, he gently brought up his plans to take a vacation. He assured her he wouldn't go far away. He planned to stay in Grandma's cabin and live off the land around the old homestead. He said he wanted peace and quiet; no electricity, no cellphones, only himself and nature.

"You plan on going native?" She asked him.

"As much as possible," he replied. "I may even run naked in the woods, who knows," he laughed.

His Mom grinned up at him then said, "for a unique experience, why don't you take a little of my peyote with you. Commune with a spirit animal and get to know which one looks after you."

Griffin had never taken drugs before. He hardly took over-the-counter meds when he had head or stomach issues, but this idea intrigued him. Indians didn't see the harm in the occasional trip with a mind-altering drug. They felt it was important to know visually what lived alongside them in a spiritual realm.

Griffin told his mom he would be leaving the next day and reminded her he wouldn't have a way for her to contact him. If something happened she was to call her friend, Lucy, who could send her husband to look for him at the cabin. He didn't want her relying on Uncle Randy anymore for anything.

Griffin was about to leave her house when she said, "son, you need to know something. It isn't as wild around Grandma's cabin anymore. You'll have to venture north of her property for hunting."

When he asked why she informed him that a few of their native friends had developed a 'Nature Tour' for the summer Indian gawkers so they could make money for the winter months.

Then she giggled and commented, "be careful out there. You don't want them gawking at your nakedness."

The Call of Nature

Jesus, Zion, and I were glad to be in the same timeframe with our assignments. It wouldn't be long before the two people met each other and we could work on getting them married like God wants. As a native searching for a reunion with nature, Griffin was about to come face-to-face with a person instead of a spirit animal.

Odette was enjoying herself eminently. Everywhere she went there were Indigenous people willing to show her their tribal culture. On her way alone, she found a brochure for a Nature Tour into the wilds and booked a trip. She wanted to know more of their former ways of life and felt a guided tour would be fun.

She packed the car with her luggage and checked out of the hotel, before driving to the Nature Tour designation. Many people were at the ride-share waiting for the tour. While waiting, she was chatting with Jesus and Zion in the cool of her car until a school bus arrived driven by a large Indian man arrived.

Before Odette opened the car door, Jesus said, "put your identifications and car fob inside your pants pocket. Only tote water and snacks in your handbag."

She took her credit cards and driver's license out of her wallet and put them in a Ziploc sandwich bag before tucking them into her pants pocket. She emptied out the contents of her bag and place everything, including her cell phone and checkbook inside the glove box. Then she threw two bags of nuts and two boxes of raisins in the bag with a large bottle of water. All she had on her person were the car fob and the sandwich bag with her personal identification and credit cards. she looked like a tourist and was glad Jesus gave her security instructions.

The bus driver stopped periodically for them to see old campsites and such. Once, when they stopped they were asked to find places to sit under a makeshift pole barn for lunch. Odette sat next to an older couple and enjoyed a traditional native dish that the tour guides furnished for their patrons.

The bus ride was over. Everyone had to walk along paths for the rest of the tour in the extreme heat. The trail was beautiful with lush vegetation and a babbling brook, but Odette couldn't enjoy the scenery. The heat caused her stomach to hurt. The lunch was not agreeing with her digestive system and she needed to use a toilet badly, but there were no facilities in the woods.

Embarrassed, she separated herself from the group and didn't even tell the couple she'd eaten lunch with that she needed to take a different path. Odette wanted and needed privacy, so she walked deep into the thick trees and bushes hoping to find a place to relieve her cramping stomach. Her plan was to do her business then walk back to the bus and wait on the others.

The vegetation was extremely thick, but Odette found a private place quickly to relieve herself. What she hadn't counted on was not being able to retrace her steps after she finished, and she got very lost and no one heard her calls for help.

Odette walked around for hours worrying if someone knew to look for her, and she grew angry with herself for not packing her cell phone. She took a break and sat on a fallen log to drink some water and gather her courage not to panic.

She jumped when she heard something scramble next to her. It was a raccoon running away with her handbag in tow. She was shocked but thanked Jesus for suggesting she take precautions with her identity. The incident proved He was one step ahead and she wasn't alone.

"Jesus, walk with me. Help me find my way back to the others," she prayed.

"I'm with you, Odette. Follow the sun and walk to a designated area," He said.

She assumed the designation was back where she got off the bus or at someone's home since Jesus said there was one, she trusted His advice. She found her handbag along the way. Nothing was left inside of it accept the napkins she used at lunch. The little thieves had stolen all her nuts and raisins. Luckily, she was drinking water when she heard the critter snatching her bag. At least she had something to gather water from a brook if she got thirsty.

Odette reverted to her old ways of babbling to Jesus instead of conversing. She talked and talked hoping He was listening. She walked slowly to reserve energy and avoid twisting an ankle. The ground was uneven, and roots were hidden by the underbrush. She managed to walk through the obstacles but did not expect a crevasse. The late afternoon shadows made it hard to see where to step and she stepped into nothingness screaming loudly all the way down into the deep pit. She landed hard and blacked out from the trauma.

Griffin had called Lucy's husband, Johnson, and asked if he would take him to the woods close to his Grandma's cabin. He wanted to make sure Johnson knew where to find him if necessary. At four o'clock the next morning, they were on the way. Johnson dropped Griffin off at a rideshare and he walked the remainder of the way to the cabin.

Griffin looked around the unkept cabin. It was evident that squirrels and raccoons had been inside. He cleaned up their mess as well as he could. Even though it was a one-room cabin it had everything he needed. It had a washbasin, a cot, pots, pans, plates, and utensils plus a fireplace to cook and stay warm by if the nights got cold.

He unpacked his gear, took off his shirt and jeans then pulled on just a pair of deerskin pants. His feet were not accustomed to soft shoes, so he put his work boots back on his feet. After he dressed, he grabbed his small backpack to store away, and the peyote he'd packed inside of it fell on the floor. He picked up the herb put it in his pocket and made the quick decision to try it later that day.

One of the first things on his agenda was to set a few traps to catch fish. He didn't want to totally rely on his rifle for food, so he looked behind the cabin and found two fish traps and a container. He'd packed a bag of jerky and thought a piece of it would work inside the traps as bait then he took all of the items to the creek. After he filled the trap's bait boxes with jerky, he tied the traps to tree limbs and threw them in the water, then he filled the container with water and walked back to the cabin to search the old garden site for vegetables and herbs. He found a few root vegetables left over from gardens a few years back and some wild asparagus. He also found a handful of blackberries and ate all the raw food for lunch. Next, he boiled some of the water and set it aside to cool so he could dip out of the pot when he got thirsty. Once he had all his chores finished, he decided to take a hike and enjoy the rest of the day. He looked in the small backpack to see what he had inside before starting the trek. There were matches, a knife, and a disposable poncho inside of it. He added the bag of jerky to snack on later, placed his wooden flute inside then picked up his rifle and began walking north in the direction his mom suggested.

Along the path, he saw rabbits, squirrels, a snake, and a skunk. They made him wonder if one of them was his spirit guide. He sat on an old fallen tree branch and pulled out the dried peyote he had in his pocket. The time was now or never, so he threw one of the buds in his mouth and chewed. The bitter taste was awful and the more he chewed the worse it got. He couldn't stand the taste. It made him gag, so he spit it out of his mouth, but the drug had gotten into his system.

His head began to spin, and he found it hard to stand, and he had to sit on the ground. Paranoia began setting in. He wanted to keep his fears under control and be like his ancestors who enjoyed the experience, so he cried out for his spirit animal and begged it to appear quickly and comfort him.

Griffin didn't like being under the drug's influence. The trees seemed to sway, animal sounds were too loud and the hair on his neck felt like it was crawling on his skin. While he waited for his spirit guide to appear, he heard a woman's scream and it snapped him out of his own fears.

Sights and Sounds Too Hard to Believe

The stage was set. We had Griffin and Odette in the same area. All we had to do was guide Griffin to where Odette lie. Even in his drugged state, Griffin would know what she needed. Medical training for animals wasn't too different than for humans.

Jesus decided He would manifest for Griffin but not talk, He would leave the communication to Zion. I planned to manifest as a wolf and swan, so Griffin wouldn't panic anymore. Between the three of us, we had a plan to carry out.

All of Griffin's senses were heightened from the peyote. His eyesight was super keen, he heard ants walking, and everything he touched or that touched him was extreme. On unsteady legs, he listened intently for the lady again.

He called out; said he was near. If she moaned he would hear where she was. Suddenly, standing in front of him was a man dressed in a white robe. He didn't speak but motioned for Griffin to follow Him. Griffin almost ran in the opposite direction until he noticed the wolf and swan from his dream standing next to the man. That's when Griffin's heart began to beat faster. He wondered if they were there to take him to his soulmate or was he completely enveloped in a hallucination? Only one way to find out the truth. The scream was female, so he began to follow the strange man. After two steps, he hears a feminine voice say, "I am Mother Nature. The man you see is your spirit guide, trust Him. The animals are there to assist Him."

The wolf ran, and the swan flew ahead of them until they came to a deep crevasse. The man dressed in white began a descent down into the earth's rift and Griffin followed His lead. At the bottom of the rift, lay one of the prettiest women Griffin had ever seen. Even in the twilight hours of the late afternoon, the sunlight caused her red hair to shine and highlighted her porcelain skin. She looked fairylike.

When he saw the lady wasn't moving, Griffin's medical training kicked into overdrive. He rushed to her side and began the vital checks to see if she were breathing. Happy to feel the air come from her nose, he ran his hands over her body to see if she had broken bones. She had a dislocated knee, nothing else out of place or broken. He rolled her over on her side and that's when he noticed a real problem. Her hair was matted with blood. She could be in extreme danger but there wasn't anything he could do for a head injury. All he could do was relocate her knee, splint the leg, keep her warm, and wait for a daybreak.

Griffin looked around for his spirit guide, but He had disappeared. The wolf and swan were also gone. Confident he had Mother Nature keeping him company, he found a little stream meandering through the crevasse. At the stream's edge, he took off his boots, removed his socks and dropped the smelly things in the water. He rinsed them out repeatedly until he was sure they didn't smell anymore and ran back to the lady. Using his wet socks, he wiped the blood from her hair and was able to see the injury better. There was a small cut, which didn't need stitching under her hair, this was good news. As gently as possible, he rotated the knee back in its proper position then he found two straight reeds and some vines to use for splints. When he finished with her medical needs, he pulled the disposable poncho out of his pack, laid down beside her and covers them, so they would be warm as they waited for daybreak when he could see how to get them out of the hole. The lady's breathing was steady, and rhythmic, so Griffin relaxed next to her until his body's tiredness kicked in and he also drifted off to sleep.

With her eyes still closed, Odette regained consciousness in excruciating pain, unable to move and feeling a warm sensation spreading under her thighs. That's when it occurred to her that she was urinating on herself.

Her eyes popped open, and that's when she saw him; a native Indian standing over her. He looked wild, so she screamed in a panic!

Griffin knelt and handed her a bottle of water, then said, "it's okay, I won't hurt you. I'm here to help. You've had a bad fall, so try not to move fast."

Odette wasn't polite. she was scared and highly embarrassed, so she snapped back, "you're not the one lying in pee with a splitting headache."

He didn't respond to her rudeness. He turned and walked away. When he returned, he knelt beside her again, helped her to sit up then handed her a long, limp piece of brush. "Chew on this, its willow bark and will relieve some of your pain," he said.

"Why do I have the splint on my leg, is it broken?" Odette asked him while she chewed on the willow bark.

He replied, "it's not broken. It was dislocated when I found you. I had to twist it back in place. The splint is precautionary because I don't want you to bend it for a day or two. You blacked out from a head injury. That's why you should take movements slow."

The willow bark was sour tasting, but it was relieving some of her pain. It also refreshed her mouth, so she used the frayed ends to brush around her teeth. Her mouth wasn't the only part of her needing refreshment. She was wet from her own pee.

She asked sweetly this time, "Sir, do you have anything I can change into? My legs are stinging from the urine."

"I'll help you undress an wash your clothes," he said.

Mortified, she said, "I'll stay the way I am. You're not helping me undress."

He laughed. "You misunderstood me. I have a poncho. You can cover up with it while I wash your clothes in the stream."

Odette agreed, but only because the urine was drawing bugs. He took a knife and cut away the vines and removed the splint. Then he helped her stand, asking her not to put weight on the leg. With his assistance, she hopped over to a bolder and sat. He removed her running shoes, helped her up again and wrapped his extra-large, plastic poncho around her waist, so it looked like a long skirt. "Undo your cargo pants and push your clothes below your knees I'll pull them off your legs." He instructed.

Odette was completely covered. So, she heeded his request and pushed the wet clothes below her knees. Once he had the wet clothes in hand, she said, "I have things in the pockets.

His eyes grew wide when he had the car fob in his hands. "You have a car nearby?" He excitedly asked her.

"It's parked at a ride-share somewhere. I was on a Nature Tour when I got separated from the crowd." She replied.

"I know exactly where the ride-share is. When I find a way out of this hole, I'll help you out. If you wish, I'll take you to a hospital," he informed.

She breathed a sigh of relief.

He looked at the baggie with her credentials and said, "I was worried for nothing. I found your handbag empty except for napkins and the water bottle, I thought you'd been mugged and pushed into this pit."

"I wasn't mugged, I stumbled into it all by myself. I only had the handbag to carry snacks and water. I was drinking water when a raccoon took the snacks but left me the bag and napkins." She joked.

With her bare butt resting on the boulder, Odette watched the man wash her pants and panties in the stream. It occurred to her they hadn't even introduced themselves. She watched his every move and began to feel the sensual stirrings in her belly again. His light caramel colored skin glistened in the sunlight. *I like the tastes of caramel,* she thought to herself. His hair was every woman's dream; thick, long, and black as pitch. Everything about him was beautiful to look at.

When he finished washing her items, he draped them over a tree branch to dry. Then he returned to her with a wet sock and a refilled water bottle.

She lowered her head to keep him from noticing her embarrassment. She wasn't in a good emotional place. Her desire to lick his flesh had made her face flush. He placed the sock on the bolder beside her and handed her the bottle, "you can wash with this sock and water from the stream. I'll leave you alone for a while. I noticed some muscadines on the other side of the stream that will be good for breakfast. I'll be back soon."

Odette was relieved to see him walk off without seeing her frustration. When he returned with the fruit she was cleaned, composed and very thankful she had someone this nice taking care of her. His good looks were only a bonus.

While they ate the sweet fruit, introductions were made, and Griffin informed her that they were not in a hole after all. There was an easy way out of the place when her knee was better. In the meantime, he planned to set up a campsite where they would be out of the elements.

Wrapped in the plastic poncho, Odette watched this hunk of a man work for hours creating a shelter. When her clothes were dry enough to wear again, he helped her dress then he took the poncho and cut it in half. One part, he lay on the shelter's makeshift floor to keep them dry, warm, and bug-free. The other half went on the top of the structure to keep them dry if it rained.

When he was finished, he helped her get inside his structure, sat down beside her, and handed her some jerky. That's when reality clicked in Odette's brain. They would be sharing the space. We heard her thoughts loud and clear. She was pleading for our help; *I'm in trouble!*

Distractions

While eating the meager lunch, Griffin couldn't help notice that Odette was an extremely beautiful woman. He found it hard to keep from glaring at her. Her light green eyes and sensuous mouth affected him greatly, and he wondered how her mouth would taste on his. When she asked him for water, his thoughts of attacking her mouth with his vanished, and knew he had to find something else to do that would keep him away from her vulnerability and innocence.

Handing Odette, the water bottle, he said, "I'll be back shortly, you'll need more willow bark soon. It will help with inflammation around your knee and keep you from hurting."

He gathered several branches of the willow bark and cut down vines to use for other projects. When he returned to the camp, Odette was asleep in the shelter. He wanted to climb in and lie beside her, but he knew that wouldn't be wise. He was too attracted to her to rest.

Griffin made a makeshift stool to use as a toilet and stationed it behind some bushes near the shelter. He also made two panels one to prop on the back of the shelter and another for the front. When Odette cried out for him, he wasn't surprised when she said she needed to relieve herself. He grabbed napkins from her bag and happily helped her hobble over the makeshift toilet.

She looked at him with appreciation. As he walked away he said, "Don't use much of the paper. Hollar when you get finished."

Odette wanted to rest on the bolder instead of crawling back inside the shelter. Her watching his every move, made Griffin uneasy, so he made an excuse to hunt. "I'm low on jerky.

I'll go over the ridge and find something for dinner. You'll be okay, I won't be far away.'

Griffin hadn't lied to Odette. He didn't go far, he just needed space to think. Taking care of a woman on his vacation was not his plan. He found a place to sit and think and the man in the white robe came to memory. Griffin closed his eyes and said a prayer. "Mother Nature, where is my spirit guide? I need help, or I may do something I regret later."

The wind began to blow, and he heard her softly say, "Call on God."

Griffin's eyes flew open at her suggestion. He knew instantly who the spirit guide was, He was the Christian God called, Jesus. Griffin thought He was a myth. He thought, *This should not be, I am an Earth Worshiper.*'

Sunlight blinked through the trees and a beautiful female silhouette appeared within the flora. Griffin thought it was Odette at first until he notices the woman's black hair. Sighing, he thought to himself, *'I don't need another woman to worry over.'*

A giggle came from the woman's direction. "I don't need anyone's help. If anything, you need mine."

"Are you Mother Nature," Griffin asked.

"I am," she replied.

Griffin stood and then knelt in awe, bowing his head, he asked, "why do you want me to trust the Christian God?"

"He is my Son, Griffin. Why wouldn't I want you to trust in Him?" She answered.

"To my understanding, Mary gave birth to Jesus," Griffin said

Her reply baffled him, "Mary agreed to be a surrogate mother for me. You see, my firstborn spirit man died, and she and Jesus were willing to give me another."

Griffin didn't know what else to say or how to ask questions. He was still in shock until he noticed the wolf and swan that came alongside her. Their appearance loosened his tongue and he quickly asked, "Are you trying to tell me that Odette Payne is my soulmate? Can she give me answers to Christianity?"

Mother Nature winked at him. Then she and the animals disappeared. Griffin grabbed his rifle and started walking back to camp when he heard Mother Nature's voice whisper from the treetops, "Don't return to camp empty-handed. A few squirrels have agreed to sustain you and Odette by giving you their bodies. Take their lives and return their spirits to me. When you see their blood, don't forget to thank them for their sacrifice.

When Griffin walked off, Odette was elated. She wanted an overdue conversation with Jesus. She had questions and wanted to know why she was in this predicament.

Behind her, Jesus said, "you want, and want. Do you even care what we want for you?"

His rebuff startled her. She said, "sorry, I am confused. I thought you cared for my well-being."

"Are you lacking anything, Odette? Are you alone? Are you really crippled?" He asked sternly.

Odette was slack-jawed by His answer, she felt ashamed of herself for complaining. She had food, water, shelter, pain reliever, beautiful scenery and an Indian Adonis taking care of her. She didn't need anything except a healthy leg.

She apologized quickly and asked, "what about my injuries? Were they part of your plan?"

"Every action has a reaction," He answered.

"What does that mean?" She inquired.

He smiled and said, "you should have told someone about your stomach issue and not just walk away from the group. Odette, we didn't plan for you to suffer. Just like your stomach, your leg will recover quickly."

Then He said, "we used your fall to get Griffin's attention. The two of you were destined to meet."

"Huh? You wanted us to meet, why?" She confusedly asked.

Zion appeared by Jesus' side and said, "didn't you beg for a mate a few weeks ago? God knows your desires before you do and hand-picked Griffin for you, sweetie. He's beautiful, isn't he? He's also a gentleman and very smart. You're having your desires met because you asked the right ones for help."

Odette had problems wrapping her brain around this news. "You want Griffin and I together?" She asked, again.

"Yep! The two of you will fit like a hand in a glove. This way you get to enjoy learning native ways and histories while exploring each other." Zion replied.

"Okay, but isn't, this all moving very fast?" Odette asked with utmost amazement.

"Not to us," Zion replied.

"What about the sin of sex before marriage?" Odette asked.

Jesus then suggested, "You are already married in God's eyes. Marriage is only a piece of paper. You can sign papers at a later date. First, entertain Griffin with your brain and not your body. Show him who you are instead of feeding his lust. It won't take long before you'll know for sure he is perfect for you. Then, you can enjoy sex with God's approval."

While they talked, Odette worked with her hands. She made a set of crutches from the vines and branches Griffin had left on the ground next to the boulders they used for chairs. She wanted to move around without someone's help. While she was trying them out, Jesus and Zion disappeared. A few seconds later, Griffin returned to camp with two squirrels in hand.

"Look at you!" Griffin said with delight.

Odette sneered at him, "I'm not a helpless bimbo. I want to do my part around here and stop relying on you to take care of me."

"How do you feel?" He asked.

"I feel fine. I've had my spirit renewed, and I chewed on more of the willow bark. Other than a sour stomach from the bitter juice, I can't complain."

Griffin held up the squirrels, "I have dinner. After I dress the meat, would you mind washing it off and spearing the meat with branches, so they can cook?"

"Sure, I can do that. Where are you going?" Odette asked.

"We need firewood and more fruit to eat." He answered.

Their conversation was light. The words felt strained, and it occurred to Odette that Griffin was sexually frustrated too.

More Than Good Looks

Seeing Odette after the discussion with Mother Nature, Griffin felt differently about her. He hadn't expected to see her walking with makeshift crutches. He had instant respect for her ingenuity, and her willingness to help him at camp intrigued him further. Odette was no ordinary woman and a desire for her rushed through his body. Griffin had to quickly find a distraction, and searching for firewood would give him time to adjust. Then making a literal fire would quench the figurative fire growing inside of his body.

He returned several times to the campsite with wood and sticks and each time, he studied Odette. She knew how to use his knife to strip bark from the branches. She halved squirrels and skewered them on the sticks. Her body movements had his mouth watering and not for the food.

Odette's charm captivated him as much as her body. He was deeply impressed when she told him she had a doctorate, even if it wasn't in medicine. He knew then, he had to make her his woman. She was everything he desired; beautiful and highly intelligent.

She had Griffin laughing through their meal. Especially when she told him how she wound up in the crevasse. Hearing that she lived in Georgia and was there to research native history had him fixated because his Great Grandparents came from Georgia. He enjoyed telling her what he knew about their lives.

Griffin hesitated when she asked about his job. It was evident to him that she liked the traditional Indian sitting with her, and he worried she wouldn't be impressed if she knew he was more like her than a native. The truth was always best, though, so he answered her question. "I am a Veterinarian and own an Animal Clinic nearby."

Odette laughed and asked why he was acting like a native. Griffin said, "I am native, and adhere to my traditions as much as possible. My mother couldn't stand it if I dressed like a typical white man. She complains I'm too white.

"You are far from being like any white guys I know," Odette giggled.

"What does that remark mean?" He asked.

"Picture pale-faced men with pudgy bodies who live off fast food. The guys, I associate with are teachers who don't go outside or have a clue how to live outdoors." She told him.

"Do you have a boyfriend back home?" Griffin asked.

"Lord, no!" I don't date.

"Why?" He frankly asked. "Are you a lesbian?"

"NO! I love men, I've been busy forming a career and getting established. I want to settle down one day and have a family. I don't like living alone." She said.

"Do you have any family in Georgia?" Griffin inquired further.

"Mom and Dad live there, but they travel a lot. Dad is fulfilling Mom's dream of seeing the world while they can. We spend more time together on our cell phones than we do at family functions. Since graduating and working in town, we connect on a regular basis at our church. Sometimes we eat lunch afterward.

When I was in college, there were months we didn't see each other. The time away from them helped me see I had to be an independent person. They weren't going to be around forever," she said."

Her answers gave Griffin hope. He only had one thing to fret and that was her establishment to teaching and having her own place in Georgia. Both being thousands of miles from him. When she answered his questions, decided to make his intentions clear.

Odette was grateful to have had her discussion with Jesus earlier. She knew how to act when Griffin returned from gathering wood and fruit. She started every conversation and kept their banter fun and enlightening. She was enjoying the company.

Learning he was a Veterinarian, impressed her. Zion wasn't kidding when she said he was smart. Hearing how he felt about his mother's feelings proved his gentle nature and love for family. Griffin was more than a handsome native man.

She noticed when Griffin relaxed, and began asking more personal questions. She answered each question as they came honestly because she didn't want assumptions or facades between them. If he was to be her intended, she wanted his trust completely.

Odette informed him she was not gay. She loved men. She also said she was ready to settle down and start a family.

When he asked about her ties to Georgia she let him know quickly they weren't tightly bound.

The next step had her baffled. How was she going to show her interest in him, other than one of friendship? How was she going to flirt without looking stupid?

She asked him the same questions he asked her, "Griffin, do you have a girlfriend back home?"

"No. I haven't found any I'd like," he said.

Odette looked into his eyes and asked, "what are you looking for?"

She was shocked to hear him say, "someone like you."

"Why me? I thought you wanted to continue in native tradition," she sweetly inquired.

"I can turn you into a squaw. You'd be the first pale-faced one in my family. I'd be a proud chief," he laughed.

"What about your mother's opinion of white people?" Odette asked.

With a weird phrase, he answered her, "she'd have to shut up or eat crow."

"What?" Odette complained.

"She's been begging me to marry someone for years. If I choose a pale-face, she will have to deal with it," he snickered.

Their playful conversations ended after his statement. Griffin kicked dirt over the fire and helped her stand then he motioned for them to go inside the shelter.

Suddenly, Odette wasn't ready for what he implied. She had to be truthful even if it meant he'd get angry with her. "Griffin, I'm not ready for sex. I've never been with a man. If we could wait, I would be most grateful." She stammered.

"You want me?" He asked.

Odette didn't hesitate, she said, "yes, just not like this. I want to feel clean and in comfortable surroundings for my first experience."

Griffin was shocked to hear she was a virgin. He replied sweetly, "We'll wait for sex. My desire is only to please you, but I can't wait to kiss you!"

Odette forgot to tell him she'd also never been kissed. Suddenly, his arms were around her and his mouth forcibly took hers. When his tongue entered her mouth, it felt like fireworks exploded in her groin. Her body quaked in his arms and she would have fainted from bliss if he hadn't held her so tightly.

Griffin knew something was different about her and stopped the kiss. Then, he grabbed her hair from behind and turned her face up so he could look into her eyes and asked, "you've never been kissed either, have you? I was your first."

Breathy, Odette sighed, and said, "you're the first. Do it again."

A gentle rain forced Griffin and Odette inside of the shelter. The three of us looked around and saw God walking up to us. He had started the rain to fall.

"Hello, everyone. Sorry to interfere, but they need privacy and rest. You can check on them later. It won't be long before they call you again." He said.

Zion quickly went to His side and said, "we have them together, finally. Notice how Griffin is treating Odette. He reminds me of you."

"Their drama has only begun, Sweetheart. They will face many trials before they can comfortably be husband and wife. Right now, they don't need us watching or listening in on their thoughts. Spirit can make sure they are okay. In a few days, they'll be ready to discuss why and what brought them together. Then they will want all of us in their lives on a regular basis." God said.

A Need for Civilization

Odette woke up and was alone in the shelter. She called out to Griffin, but he did not answer. Before she slid out into the open to find him, she rubbed her fingers over her mouth. Their kissing had been intense, and her lips felt bruised. She also remembered the exhilaration in her loins from the first one.

Griffin didn't force anything else on Odette ance they entered the shelter, he just made sure it wasn't going to leak. Satisfied they were going to stay dry, he stretched out next to her, drew her into his arms and kissed her on the forehead instead of on the mouth again. She was a little disappointed when he said, "Odette, the rain distracted me enough to calm my passion. I don't want to stay frustrated all night. Let's listen to the rain as it beats softly on the plastic above our heads and try to get some sleep."

Odette didn't argue with him one bit. She'd been uncomfortable too, so she laid her head on his chest and closed her eyes and listened to the rain. The rain wasn't what made her sleepy, it was the steady beat of Griffin's heart that soothed her worries away. When his arms tugged her body closer, all her fears of rejection fled, and she quickly fell asleep.

Odette quietly slid out of the shelter and looked around the campsite. Her heart skipped a beat when she saw Griffin climbing out of the stream. He didn't know she was looking. Her eyes were fixed on his wet, rippling muscles. He looked like a god coming from the water. She'd seen pictures of naked men before, but nothing compared to the beauty that stood a few feet in front of her. She couldn't believe that this man wanted her the night before and she had said 'no' to his advances.

After he slipped back into his pants, he began to wring the water from his hair. Odette still hadn't moved or made a sound, she could stare at him for days. Every movement he made was sensual and had her heart beating fast.

To calm her nerves, she sat slowly on the boulder and continued to watch him from the perch. It was obvious that he wasn't in a hurry to return to their campsite. With his back to her, she watched him pick up a wooden reed and was surprised it was a flute when he began to play. His music was sweet and romantic. It was nothing like the pounding beats of the tribal drums that entranced her before in Georgia.

Odette wanted to be near him as he played, so she slowly hobbled over to the stream and sat next to him by the water's edge. "Your music is beautiful," she said.

"Thanks, did I wake you up?" He asked.

She answered truthfully, "I've been up awhile. I saw you climb out of the water. I wish I could bathe, I feel grubby."

He snickered, "I didn't go into the cool water to bathe, Odette. If I hadn't run into the water, I would have raped you!"

Shocked by his statement, she shyly said, "Griffin, I want you too. I just want my first experience to be nice for both of us. Not when I smell and feel unattractive. Please respect my wishes."

He leaned over to her, took her face in his hands, and kissed her lightly. "I get it, Odette. You don't want to rut like an animal. I don't either, that's why I cooled down in the stream."

"What are your plans today?" Odette asked, changing the subject.

"If you can walk, we'll try and make it back to my cabin. If not, I'm running to get your car. There is a road close by," he answered.

Odette stood and placed weight on her leg with a crutch under her arm for stability. Pressure on the leg hurt a lot. With a grimace on her mouth, she said, "I can't yet. Just standing on it hurts."

"Then I'll be running after we eat breakfast if you can manage without me for an hour or so," he said

"I have all I need. I'll be okay until you return." Then her stomach growled, "are there any more grapes? I can't wait for you to hunt something to eat. I'm ready for you to run after the car," she confessed.

"Jerky and grapes, a meal for champions." He answered.

They finished the bag of jerky and remaining grapes from dinner the night before. Griffin refilled the bottle of water and left her to fend for herself. While he was gone, she hobbled over to the make-shift toilet. While there, she wondered if natives used such stools in the 1800's. She hadn't recalled such in her studies, but something given Griffin the idea to build one. She banked that question for later because she wanted to learn everything about his culture. She had to if she was going to be his 'squaw.'

Griffin ran as fast as he could to the ride-share. There were four cars parked there. He took Odette's car fob and pressed the locator feature. When a jeep's taillights flashed, he was impressed with his woman's taste in cars. She liked utility vehicles instead of flashy rides.

As soon as he entered the vehicle Griffin remembered Odette saying she had placed her cell phone in the glovebox. He pulled it out, along with its mobile charging cord, and plugged them in to charge while the motor ran. There were four calls in her voice mail. He knew they had to be from her parents because she said they talked almost every day.

Griffin thought of calling Lucy to ask if she would send someone to clean his apartment but decided against it. Odette wanted her first experience to be nice, so he called his secretary and asked her to book the best room at the Governor, the town's hotel. He'd make it a romantic experience. The room had a Jacuzzi and wet bar fully stocked, they could bathe together and relax with wine and order good meals from room service.

Once the evening plans were set, Griffin pulled out of the ride-share and drove to his Grandma's cabin, changed clothes, and gathered his gear. Then he drove north, close to where he felt the campsite would be to get Odette.

Griffin found the campsite quickly where Odette staying busy making a basket from the vines he had placed around the site. He studied her for a few minutes before rushing down into the crevasse. Even disheveled, she was a beautiful sight for his eyes. He could easily ravage her body just the way she was, but he wanted to make love to all of her; spirit, soul, and body.

Out of nowhere, a pang of guilt entered his heart. He was taking her somewhere he'd visited often with another woman.

Briefly, he thought about changing venues, but he didn't know of a better place to show Odette a good time.

He'd met Lois Jones, an Indian lady, after receiving money from his Dad's stocks. She worked at the bank he used and thought she was attractive. Griffin knew after only a few dates that she was not his soulmate, she was too wild and adventurous, so he used her just for sex.

Just about every weekend after meeting her, they'd meet at the hotel to enjoy each other. With Lois, Griffin could be an animal. .He could enjoy her body without any emotional commitment and he felt like she used him the same way. He didn't want that kind of relationship with Odette. He was looking forward to teaching her the pleasures of lovemaking and molding her to his personal needs.

With lust surging through his body again, Griffin rushed down the embankment and his sudden movements scared Odette bad enough to make her scream with fear.

"It's me, Odette!" He yelled.

"I thought you were a bear or some other large animal. I almost had a heart attack," she yelled back at him.

He hugged her close and kissed her softly, then asked, "are you ready to be carried up the hill? Your car isn't far from here."

She blushed and said, "I don't like being a burden, but I can't climb with these crutches. You'll have to help me because my hands and armpits are raw from the rough bark."

"Shut up!" He said, then threw her over his shoulders like a firefighter and began the climb up to the road above. Griffin carried her until he couldn't take another step. He gently placed her on her feet and pointed her towards the jeep that wasn't far away from them. From there, she managed to make the few yards to the jeep without hurting herself further from the crutches.

She noticed right away that Griffin had her cell phone charged, and she began to listen to her messages. Like he had suspected, the calls were from her parents. It impressed him to hear her talk with them. Instead of giving them reasons to worry about her health and well- being, she told them a vague truth, saying she had accidentally misplaced the phone and she had just found it again.

After their conversation, he asked, "why didn't you tell them everything?"

Her answer was sweet. "There is no need for them to worry about me. My knee will be better soon, and I have everything I need. Why give them more grey hair?'

Griffin had the car in motion and showed her where the ride-share had been from their campsite. Then he drove them to town. When he stopped the jeep in front of the hotel, she looked confused. He eased her mind, "I'm not taking you to the hospital or to my place. I live like a pig and other than your knee, you seem fine. You wanted a nice place to stay, so I booked a suite."

"Are you leaving me here?" She wanted to know.

"Not alone. I still have a week or two left of my vacation before I need to return to reality," he replied.

Griffin left Odette in the jeep and went inside to get the card keys to their room. At the information desk, the clerk asked if his lady friend would like her usual meals sent to the room.

Griffin didn't tell him about Odette, he just said they would be wanting food soon and would call the kitchen after they decided.

He pulled the jeep around to the back of the building and carried Odette to the elevator. They were riding up to the top floor when she said the hotel was lovely. Griffin could hardly wait for her to see the inside of their room.

He carried her to the room, opened the door, and stepped over the threshold still holding Odette in his arms. He had the pleasure of seeing her eyes twinkle and her face go pale. He realized she was scared, so he placed her on the bed and left the room to gather her suitcase and his gear, so she could compose herself.

Griffin knew when he went outside that he'd made a good impression on Odette. Since the stage was set for a romantic evening it was up to him not to rush her first experience, but prove to her that proper lovemaking was worth waiting for. He could hardly wait to make Odette his.

Connecting

It is important for me to show how both of these beautiful people experience their union, so I will share their thoughts separately where no thought or emotion is hidden or misconstrued.

Odette was dumbfounded. Griffin had heard her plea booked a lovely honeymoon suite just for them. The place was exquisite.

To her surprise, this wild-man she'd fallen for was a gentleman through and through. He hadn't forced anything. Soon after they entered the room, he sat her gently on the huge bed, kissed the top of her head and said he would be back with the luggage. He was giving her time to adjust, but Odette could hardly wait for him to return.

She turned to look around the room and noticed a mirror on one side of the bed. She gasped at her reflection. She looked wild. With a bruise on her cheek, grass in her hair, and dirt all over her clothes she looked horrible. She was a mess and couldn't believe Griffin wanted her the way she looked.

She jumped off the bed and hobbled into the bathroom. The room was divine there was even a large Jacuzzi to soak in. She wanted to get in it but thought better of it. Instead, she washed her face and was trying to pick the grass and twigs out of her hair when Griffin returned with their luggage.

"Odette?" He whispered.

She came out of the bathroom to see two wine glasses in his hands. Playfully, she asked, "you plan to get me drunk, chief, so you can have your way with me?"

"Wine will make you relax. I'm in no hurry," he answered.

Odette was glad he didn't know how frustrated she was. All her worries faded when she looked into his eyes and understood he was patiently waiting for her to make the first move. She nodded towards the bathroom and said, "I can't wait to bathe. I could use someone to help me into the tub. Want to join me?"

She trembled with need as he helped her completely undress and get into the warm bubbling water. The second she was completely in, she ducked under the soapy water and began scrubbing her hair. She wanted to look better when he came in the water alongside her. As soon as his foot brush her leg, she came up for air to see him standing in all his naked glory holding the two goblets filled with wine in his hands.

He handed her the glasses so he could sit in the water. Then he said to her, "drink, Odette. Allow the wine to ease your tension. I want you completely relaxed"

Odette nervously drank the glass of wine too fast. He poured her another from the bottle he'd placed beside the tub, and said, "relaxed, Odette, not drunk!"

Her senses were overloaded. Everything she knew about lovemaking didn't compare with being in its grasp. Griffin wooed her tenderly and carried her over the sensual edge many times while they bathed each other in the Jacuzzi.

They were thoroughly clean and relaxed when he helped her out of the bath. Wrapping a warm towel around them, he began to dry her from head to toe. He didn't want her to do anything, so she glared at him drying their bodies.

Griffin scooped up her dry body and carried her to the large bed, covered himself with the necessary precaution and took her virginity as gently as he could. The experience was painful, but she'd never been so happy, she felt like a complete woman responding to his movements. After experiencing bliss, both drifted off to sleep minutes later.

It was an hour or so later when Odette woke up feeling Griffin kissing her belly and hearing him whispering something in an Indian dialect. She knew at this moment she was completely in love with this man. To see his face, she brushed her hands through his thick black hair and it caused him to look up at her.

"Did I hurt you, Odette?" He asked.

"A little at first, but then I couldn't get enough of you," she answered.

Without saying another word, he slid off the bed and gathered her into his arms, and took her back inside the bathroom. Standing in from of the mirror she saw why he asked if he hurt her. Griffin attentively washed the blood from her groin and legs. Odette expected more sex, but instead of making love to her again, Griffin wrapped her in a luxurious robe that was provided by the hotel. Then he helped her back into the bedroom so they could order a huge meal and more wine.

Soon after Griffin return to the room, he poured two glasses of wine, then called her name. He was ready when she came out of the bathroom. What she said next caught him off guard. He'd expected her to want a few minutes by herself to freshen up then eat a late lunch, he couldn't believe his ears when she wanted him to bathe with her so soon.

In the bright light of the bathroom, Griffin watched this shy, lovely woman pretend to be sexy but instead, she trembled at his touch. Watching her body become sexually stimulated from the bares touch was very erotic to him than anything Lois ever did to turn him on.

Odette's skin mesmerized him. She was porcelain white all over and turning a dusty rose color; flushed with heat. She reminded him of the lovely swan in his dreams who was white with pink undertones.

He moved slowly and enjoyed unwrapping his present. He didn't want her to think he wanted a quick fix. He helped her safely sit on the edge of the Jacuzzi and handed her the soap and shampoo. Then he watched her slide into the water and duck underneath while he undressed.

She wasted no time washing the grime off her face. She was underwater scrubbing her hair when he stepped into the bath with their goblets of wine. The water nymph before him was beautifully trying to act sensual. She was unaware that her innocence was perfect.

After she gulped her first glass of wine, Griffin quickly poured her another. Her nervous passions were coming alive, and he didn't want her drunk. Her smoldering eyes spoke volumes to him. He knew she was on fire for him again and wanted to feel the pleasures from last night's first kiss flow through her again. \

He enjoyed watching her writhe with pleasure from him simply kissing her. Seeing her respond to other touches had him wanting her even more. So, he helped her out of the bath and quickly placed her on the bed. It was his turn to writhe.

Before losing his senses to sexual pleasure, Griffin used a precaution against pregnancy then he entered her body slowly. He'd never been with a virgin before and didn't know how he'd react if she cried out in pain from the intercourse.

He felt her tense but then respond to his movements. With their lovemaking completed, they held each other and drifted off to sleep instead of ordering lunch.

Griffin slept at first until his growling belly overtook the need to sleep. He eased up on one arm to look at Odette and saw the blood. It alarmed him until he heard a gentle whisper from Zion, "Remember the squirrels?"

He wanted to cry. The beautiful woman he'd ravaged a few hours ago had sacrificed her innocent maidenhood to be his woman. It was a precious part of a woman's body and she could never get back. He was extremely honored and realized he was in love with this woman.

He kissed Odette's stomach and said a prayer of thanks to this dead part of her. In his native tongue, he committed his life to her vowing that he wanted her for his queen. He had experienced her body, she'd given him her soul, and now he needed her heart. He wanted her to give away her princess status with no worries and live with him forever.

He was lovingly snapped out of the reverence by Odette playing with his hair. He asked right away, "did I hurt you?"

Her answer melted his heart. All he could think of after her confession, was to wash away the evidence of her sacrifice then make sure she knew how precious she is to him.

She clung to him while he washed her. He could have taken her again but knew he shouldn't. because it was time he made love to her heart. Instead of stimulating her, he wrapped her in a nice robe and took her to a couch where they ordered food and wine and talked for hours.

They Want To Know Us

Zion apologized to us for whispering into Griffin's ear. Jesus answered, "You touched his heart, that's all that matters. It brought reverence to their love-making, so there is no need to apologize."

I asked Him, "what's our next step?"

"We use what presents itself and go with God's flow," Jesus replied.

Zion comments, "There is a television in the room. Why don't we urge them to turn it on and watch shows of our choosing?"

"What a great idea, we'll use Odette's interest in the Bible's truths to introduce ourselves to Griffin," Jesus exclaimed. "We'll guide her ears to a program where a Minister is speaking about love. She will want to talk with Griffin about the subject and ask us to join them. Interacting with both instead of separately is the way God wants."

We patiently waited until the two love-birds finished their meals, combed each other's hair, and climbed back into bed to relax. When Odette tried to initiate more love-making, Griffin sweetly declined and told her she needed a break. She would be sore.

It was cute to hear her beg, but Griffin didn't want to risk hurting her further. So, he turned on the television and it instantly had her attention. Her attention reverted to the Minister saying God was love.

Zion knew her cue and whispered again in Griffin's ear, "Ask her about Jesus. You wanted to know if he is a myth."

"Odette, will you answer a question for me?" He asked her.

"If I can," she said.

"Do you believe in this Jesus? My ancestors say He is a myth," Griffin questioned.

Odette smiled at him, and said truthfully, "Jesus is the only person I truly count on. He is my spiritual partner, my best friend, and instructor."

"You act as if He is flesh and blood," Griffin smirked.

Odette reacted swiftly, "He is all things, Griffin! I know Him personally. I wouldn't lie to you."

"How can you have a personal relationship with someone who died two-thousand years ago?" Griffin questioned.

Odette countered, "why do Indians claim the earth is alive?"

Griffin said, "touche! I think I understand."

To soothe Griffin's feathers, Odette said, "I know your Mother Earth personally as well. She is great."

Griffin's eyes grew wide from Odette's confession. "You know her? You've seen her for yourself?"

"Yes, Griffin. I've seen her, talked with her, and allowed her to teach me." Odette firmly stated.

Excited to hear this, Griffin admits, "I thought I saw Jesus the afternoon your fell in the crevasse, but I was under the influence of peyote. I know I saw and talked with Mother Earth the afternoon I brought squirrels to camp. She's who told me to follow Jesus, and said He was my spirit guide. She also said if I had any questions to seek the truth from you. I forgot to ask you any questions once I returned to camp. Other urges took over my brain."

Odette started laughing, "you use peyote? I heard it gives hallucinations."

"Mom twisted my arm. She said I would get in touch with an animal who would be my spirit guide throughout my life. Instead, the stuff made me sick and scared. I puked my guts up and had to lean on a tree for support and frightened out of my mind. It was your yell that forced me panicking. As I rushed to where I heard you scream, that's when I saw a man dressed in a white robe. He showed me where to find you." Griffin answered.

"Really! Jesus showed Himself to you, just for me?" Odette asked.

"Like I said, I was under the influence of peyote. I'm not sure it was Him. I only assumed." Griffin answered.

Odette took Griffin's hands and said, "I don't know if what I want will work, but it is worth a try. Don't get alarmed, I have your hands."

Odette prayed, "Jesus, you and Zion told me if I ever wanted you near I only had to ask. I'm asking now that you show this man I love who you really are."

Griffin's heart soared when he heard Odette say he was the man she loved. He focused more on her than her request until a soft breeze entered their room. Then he became dumbfounded and a little spooked.

"Greetings," Jesus said.

"Hello again, Griffin, and to you also, Odette," Zion states.

Odette looked over at Griffin. He'd gone pale. Shaking his hands, she said to him, "Griffin, I told you they were real. All you must do is believe with all your heart and they come. There is nothing to fear."

Zion also came to Griffin's rescue, "Son, you are never alone. You may not recognize us from time-to-time, but our presence is always nearby. There is no love greater than our love for creation."

Griffin shyly addresses, Jesus, "Why haven't you been angry with me? Or towards my family? We were told you were a myth, that Mother Nature was our god."

Jesus didn't hesitate to answer Griffin, "I am always forgiving. I understand why religion is confusing."

Zion looked Griffin directly in the eye, "The grey matter between your ears was not intended to rule, neither is your muscle. God and I never wanted you to fret over life for yourself or your mother. You took on a heavy load forced on you by your family since you were twelve.

We have always been here to help. Jesus understands why you didn't know to ask for help. The traditions of men screw-up things. Allow Him to hold the reigns of life from now on. All you have to do is ask for His help, live your life, and be happy."

"How?" Griffin softly asked. "My feet have been held to a flame for so many years. All I know to do is work and make sure my mother's needs are met."

It was my turn to speak, "lean on me, Griffin."

"Who are you? Where are you?" He shouted.

I entered the room the only way he could understand. I stood before him as the wolf that speaks, "I've been assigned to comfort you, pray for you, and give you strength when you feel weak. My presence will steady your emotions and help you react appropriately to life's trials and tribulations. Occasionally, I will advise you, but only with promptings from God or Jesus."

Jesus cleared His throat and said to Zion and me, "I think we have overwhelmed Griffin with our presence. Odette can answer any questions he may have for now."

Odette still held Griffin's hands in hers and squeezed them hard to bring his thoughts back to earth after we left. She whispered, "Griffin, I'm here. You are not losing your mind. This experience has just brought us closer together to show us that Jesus is the unbreakable glue connecting us to God's love.

The Trials Begin

Griffin drifted into a trance. He had many questions about his past, but he held those inside his heart for another time, when he could be alone with Jesus. On the other hand, Odette could help him understand basic, Christian beliefs. The timing was off, though. He didn't want to waste precious time in a book when he could be teaching his new teacher the arts of loving and being loved.

Odette asked, "are you okay, Griffin? Is there some way I can help you understand what just happened?'

Rolling her onto her back and pinning her hands on each side of her head, and straddled her, he said, "everything is perfect. We have all our lives to make sense of various beliefs. For now, it is my job is to show you pleasure and teach you ways to pleasure me while we are in this lovely place."

Griffin didn't want to leave Odette alone very much until she could prove she could stand without pain. He only left their room once to buy more pregnancy protection. The rest of the time, he stayed close to her, so he could tote her around the room and allow her arms, and hands to heal from using the crutches. For two days they only dressed in robes when room service or the janitors had to enter their room. They were sexually insatiable.

On the outside of their room, rumors were flying. Lucy couldn't keep her mouth shut. She told Griffin's Mom, Irene, that he wasn't in the woods anymore. That he had called and asked her to use the company's credit card to reserve the best room at the Governor for two people.

Irene was very happy to hear the news from Lucy. She knew Griffin was seeing Lois because prior gossip about her dating him was spreading swiftly. The news forced Irene to investigate the lady one day. She went to the bank where Lois worked. She introduced herself to Lois and approved of Griffin's choice. Irene thought Lois was a smart and beautiful Indian lady who would compliment their family. She was independent and had stability.

Irene hoped for a miracle since Griffin wasn't staying at his Grandma's cabin anymore. Hopefully, he'd made a decision to get married to this girl and start a family.

For two days, there wasn't another word from Lucy. Irene called Griffin's cell phone but there was no answer. The frustration of not knowing anything made her anxious.

Irene's anxiety spilled over to the wrong person when Randy asked her to have lunch with him. After driving by the hotel and not seeing Griffin's truck, she drove over to his apartment. His truck hadn't moved. It was still sitting in the parking lot where he'd parked it several days earlier.

Irene drove to the bank and went inside to get money for lunch and saw Lois on the job. Something didn't add up. Instead of confronting Lois, Irene complained to Randy which created a problem.

Griffin and Odette played like children during lunch. They had food fights with intense sexual role-playing afterward that ended with Griffin rushing to the bathroom when the love-making session ended.

Behind the closed door, Griffin examined the broken pregnancy protection and he began to worry. He washed his hands and looked in the mirror at his shocked face. Was he ready for fatherhood? Did he want a new life married to Odette?. He weighed each question and came to an immediate decision. If life was with Odette, he was a blessed man. While Odette was in the bathroom, Griffin made the decision not to say anything about the failed protection but to ask her to marry him instead.

"Odette, are you happy with me?" Griffin asked.

Her answer was quick, "I've never known life to be this good. Why?"

"Will you make it permanent? When I was in the bathroom earlier, I asked myself if I could live without you, and I realized, I don't think I can." Griffin stammered.

"What are you saying?" She asked.

"Marry me, Odette!" He shouted.

Odette didn't know what to say. In her heart, she felt they already were married. Had been assured even.

"I feel like we are already married," she answered truthfully.

Griffin asked, "really? So, you don't need a wedding?"

"I don't need a wedding, but my parents may not like it that their only child doesn't want a big show," she replied.

"Let's go to the Courthouse and get the papers, then we can have a ceremony later for your parents. I need you tied to me, today," he confessed.

"What about your mother,won't she mind? I'd mind if you were my son," Odette questioned.

"You're right, it's time you met my Mom. We'll ask her to be present when we marry. Let's get moving on this. Take a shower and put on your finest clothes while I make an appointment with the Magistrate Judge.

In the spirit realm, where we watched over them, Zion was thrilled when Odette dawned on makeup and then chose the outfit she helped her pick at the mall. Odette even added accessories; a charm bracelet and earrings that were family heirlooms. We all agreed Odette would be a lovely bride, dressed in beautiful earth tones.

It made us happy to see Griffin's face when Odette limped into the room wearing her new clothing. He looked dumbstruck and thought his fairy had turned into a goddess he would die for.

With a light nudge from me, I urged Griffin to dress just as fine, but he didn't have the proper clothes in the hotel room.

This meant he would have to show Odette his apartment and where she would soon be living. Her new abode.

"Odette, you are a goddess! I can't marry you wearing any of the clothes I have here. We'll have to go to my apartment. Do you mind?" Griffin asked.

"We're really getting married, today?" Odette asked.

Griffin smiled and said, "I made the appointment for 4:30 this afternoon. If we hurry to my apartment, I can change clothes. It will also give us time to pick up Mom. We'll check out of this room tomorrow," he said.

Odette laughed when she entered Griffin's apartment. "You really do live like a pig, Griffin. As soon as we can, we will have to make your place at least livable," she stated.

"My dear, this is your place to do with as you please. You can make it a better place for both of us until we find something better," he countered.

Griffin showered quickly and chose clothes to compliment Odette's outfit. He chose something that would make his mother happy; a deer shin suit and a pair of moccasins.

Griffin wasn't prepared for what was to come. His mother wasn't herself. She was a little tipsy from her lunch with Randy and sitting in the living room confused when they arrived. When he introduced her to Odette and told Irene that she was from Albany, Georgia, Irene began screaming in Creek, unaware that Odette knew some of the Creek Indian languages.

Hurt by Irene's disapproval, Odette fled, limping to her car to weep.   Inside the house, Griffin managed to calm his mother, but only a little by telling her she may soon be a grandmother. While still in the house, he made her promise her not to say anything to Odette about the broken contraceptive.

He coaxed her to dress and attend the wedding, but we read Irene's heart and understood she was very unhappy and planned to ruin their marriage. Her emotions said she could live with Griffin's child if one manifested, but she refused to accept a white woman from Georgia as her daughter-in-law.

Murderous Intents

Odette was shocked when Griffin opened the back door of the car for his mother. She was shocked even more to hear Mrs. Waters apologize for her behavior. But, Odette nor Griffin knew what we read in Irene's heart. She harbored murderous thoughts. We knew she hated Odette only because Griffin said she was from Georgia. Irene felt it was the ultimate insult to her mother's memory for their marriage to take place, because her mother's ancestors once lived, and some had been slaughtered, in Georgia.

The ceremony only lasted a few minutes. Afterward, Griffin wanted to treat his two favorite women to a luxurious dinner. Behind the scenes, another sinister plan was taking place.

Randy continued drinking after having lunch with Irene. He was celebrating that she agreed to eat lunch and have a few beers with him. To him, that meant she was over their indifference and wanted him in control of her life again. When she confided to him that she worried about Griffin, he thought this gave him permission to find her son. In his drunken state of mind, he decided to play 'flush out the rabbit.' If Griffin was hiding from Irene, he would flush him out the only way he could, and that was by setting fire to something Griffin owned. Griffin could afford to have it repaired.

Randy waited for Lucy to leave the Animal Clinic so he wouldn't harm her, but he was unaware there were two other people inside when broke a window and threw a Molotov cocktail inside the clinic's office. The flames rushed quickly through the office. One of the Veterinarians rain outside to get a water hose and tried to stop the fire while the other called the fire department. They worked hard to keep the fire away from the animals. Both men tried to save the office but felt it more important to protect the animals. When Randy saw their efforts, he guiltily confessed to the deed and began to help, but by the time the fire department arrived, the office was destroyed and the two Veterinarians turned the drunken Randy over to the police.

It was during his wedding dinner when Griffin received a call from the Police Station. What was to be one of the happiest days of his life had just turned into a nightmare thanks to Randy. With hatred in his heart for his uncle, Griffin hurriedly ended their meal and drove them to the clinic where he saw the results of Randy's deed.

Griffin checked on his employees was thankful they and the animals weren't hurt. When he walked up to the police officer, who had Randy in custody, he had no sympathy for the crying Randy, who was begging for mercy.

Griffin confronted Randy and demanded why he should be merciful. The drunken Randy pointed his finger towards Irene and said she couldn't find Griffin. So, he had no choice but to flush Griffin into the open. This enraged Griffin further and he angrily asked the police to take Randy away. He would press charges against him tomorrow.

Furious that his mother was also involved with this crime, he confronted her in the car for answers. Griffin's angry growls caused her to weep. Irene confessed to confiding in Randy during lunch that day and admitted she was worried about him when he wouldn't answer her calls.

With every ounce of strength Griffin could muster, he calmed his anger so he could talk to his mother. Then he explained that he hadn't been near his cell phone until that afternoon when he dressed for the wedding. Then he walked away and left her crying, so he could talk with the firemen. Griffin was so angry he wanted to wring his mother's neck for involving Randy again in their lives.

The Fire Chief told Griffin there wouldn't be anything he could do until the next day. Rather than hanging around to watch them work, he took his mother home and he and Odette went back to the hotel.

Their honeymoon night was ruined. Odette was experiencing firsthand another side of Griffin. He was in a dark place inside of his mind because of his family and was in no mood for romance. All he ranted about his mother's need to control his life, and how he felt about his Uncle Randy. Griffin's words scared Odette, especially when he said he wished Randy was dead.

Royal Hissy Fit

Jesus and I have been through this scenario many times in the past, where the issues of life overshadow any promise we'd given someone. We were prepared to ride out the drama and be available if we were called on for help, but Zion hadn't been trained to wait things out. This was her first field trip with us. All she comprehended were Odette's tormented thoughts and Griffin's raging anger as they unfolded.

When Odette went to the bathroom to cry, the ground under our feet began to shake. It swiftly dawned on us that Zion's emotions were about to explode, the same as Odette's tears.

Trying to calm the potential storm, Jesus asks, "Zion, are you okay?"

"No! Odette is in trouble and Griffin is an idiot, he doesn't even see her fears. He's too caught up in self-pity. We need to do something!" She shouts.

"We have to be patient, Zion," Jesus exclaims.

Glaring at him angrily, with her eyes flaming like a fire, Zion counters, "for what? Until they no longer have self-confidence, self-worth, or faith? I know what that is like and I don't want that for my children."

"Zion, calm down," Jesus said softly.

"Don't Zion, me! Don't tell me to calm down! You've never been chained. You've never had your ears and mouth bound, so you couldn't hear or speak. Don't try to calm me down, boy! Until you've been enslaved by a cruel master and tortured for hundreds of years, separated from your husband, and fooled into thinking your children didn't care about you or their father, don't talk to me."

I asked her, "Zion, what can we say to ease your mind?"

Crying, she said, "I don't know. I just can't stand around without intervening. They can't see the wall that has come between them. They were very happy a few hours ago. They believed in us enough to marry. One of us must wake them up!"

Quietly, Jesus cried out to Abba for help. Hearing Zion confess to us that she was worried made Him understand what was really happening. Zion was vulnerable even with us standing right beside her. Doubts and fears, especially where her earthly sons and daughters were concerned had her emotions on edge. It was evident to us that she had been away from Abba for too long. Her personal harmony depended on having Him close enough to touch or she would take things into her own hands and make matters worse. We knew this from times past. Sometimes, Satan would trap her and make her his slave when she ventured away from Abba and did things alone. A few times her enslavement lasted for centuries. Jesus couldn't risk her stepping into another demonic trap.

Micro-seconds after Jesus cried out to Abba, we heard a thunderous roar overhead, and the air around us grew thick. Whenever God leaves heaven swiftly, the spiritual environment changes drastically and forces everything in heaven and on earth to take notice.

Zion's mouth dropped open and her eyes grew bright with tears of love when she saw God. He was standing before her with His sword unsheathed, and she fell apart with gratitude.

"My Love! Thank you for coming to the rescue. Odette and Griffin are falling into Satan's trap. I can't stand to watch," Zion cried.

Abba took Zion's face in His hand forcing her to look at His face. Then He said sternly, "we have Satan in prison. He is not to blame for this. Why are you doubting my plans?"

"I'm scared! I don't have the faith you gave Jesus. I shouldn't have come on this field trip," she confessed.

Abba's heart broke. His sympathetic nature forgave Zion instantly, "Zion, my dear, I don't expect you to live by faith. You have my love.

Remember the day I planted a vineyard and said it was for Griffin and Odette? That made you sing, Then I encouraged you and Jesus to water them with hope and love and watch them grow. Nothing can destroy what I plant, or what I call into being. Even if they give us problems with worries, we must not get angry. Even ugly plants can bear good fruit."

"Why shouldn't we intervene or get angry with them? They'll tear each other apart if they ignore each other's feelings. They are too much like me; vulnerable to life's issues. I don't want that for them," Zion said.

Abba sighed, "I know why you feel this way. Creation itself is hard. You are the first one to experience the pain and chaos of love. True love is forged by fire, it goes through a lot before it is mature. True love is undeniable. Hotter than any flame and brighter than any light. We must give these two the same experience or they won't be grateful to have each other to lean on. They'll stay trapped in sexual gratification and nothing can survive on sex alone."

When Zion breathed deeply and sighed, all of us relaxed a bit. "This will be hard for me to watch," she confesses.

"I never said this would be easy for them. They were taught by outside forces how to be adults, we were never allowed to intervene. They weren't shown how to take responsibility for each action or how to stay calm during hard times. Their flesh can't accomplish that alone. You know that from experience.

Griffin and Odette can't figure out the issues alone and what they were taught by parents or traditions have failed them. They must call on Jesus for guidance. He and Spirit can show them how to walk by His faith in us. Spirit can explain how my promises combined with your wisdom and nurturing will help them through every hardship," Abba states.

"How do I nurture them through this when I can hardly control my own emotions?" Zion inquires.

"Treat the process like an illness or a garden overgrown with weeds. Take each negative reaction they make as if it were a weed that must be plucked. Deal with the action, not the person. You can destroy negativity by bringing it into the open and forgiving the person for their action. After that, you can teach them the proper discipline of clinging to me for safety. They will learn that a good and whole life is centered around our love and supports instead of conviction.

I promise the days are coming when they will know the truth, but it will take going through hard times before they develop a strong relationship. Like I stated earlier, life is not all about sex or living with ease and grandeur. Lifestyles like that are built on pretense and it's an unlivable state of mind for our human children." Abba explained in His nurturing way.

"You have a lot of confidence in me. I appreciate that you want me to try. Promise me you will stay close or I won't be able to do this correctly. Help me," Zion said shyly.

Laughing at her shy request, Abba encourages, "all you have to do is love them. Jesus has everything anchored down; for you and them. Even you must look to Him as the calm example, who lived through all the tests and passed.

During their time of testing, you will have to accept and love each of them differently. Odette will need delicate treatment, with sympathy to overcome the lies she's been taught. Griffin will need tough love. He is an angry person who must be threshed like wheat for him to work with Jesus and His angels and not fight against me. With Spirit nearby to explain details to him later, my ways will correctly be understood."

Jesus spoke next to Zion, "you'll need a big box of tissues. You'll cry a lot. Practicing patience is painful and disturbing, but together we will get through it. I won't let you fret. I'll call Abba anytime I see you sweat."

"That's good to know. Thanks," Zion answered.

Pain, Panic, and Problems

Once Abba assured Zion He would remain close, we turned our attention back to Odette and Griffin. Griffin was on his cell phone making calls and worrying about his business. Odette was in the bathroom soaking in the Jacuzzi, her knee hurt and was swollen from walking too much that day without her crutches. They were both in pain and weren't attentive to each other.

Neither spoke before going to bed and they tossed and turned all night. Nightmares had them both in the grips of torment. A nightmare woke Griffin and he refused to go back to sleep. In a panic, he dressed and called a cab. Early the next morning, the pain in Odette's knee jarred her awake. When she opened her eyes, Griffin was gone. She was alone in bed and had to deal with two types of pain; emotional and physical.

It's 1:00 a.m. in the morning when a nightmare woke Griffin. He took the nightmare as an omen from Mother Nature and swiftly heeded the message. In his dream, he was shown a small spark igniting a raging fire that would burn the remaining parts of his business to the ground, destroying everything including the kennels where he held the pets.

Griffin struggled with the thought of waking Odette. Instead of waking her, he decided to let her rest and called a cab. Dressing quickly in the bathroom, he wrote a quick note and left it on the dresser for her to find, then he went downstairs to wait for the cab.

By 2:00 a.m., Griffin had his truck and was at the clinic. Crime scene tape was crisscrossed on the front door, but he didn't let it keep him from going inside. The power had been turned off, and he had to dig around the office for a flashlight. When he had a light shining in the room, he felt like screaming. Everything was either charred or wet. His life's work was ruined.

He didn't have filing cabinets for the records, he used opened bookshelves to stack things for quick usage, so all the handwritten records had turned to ashes. His two computers were partially melted from the fast-fueled fire, and without them, he had no way of knowing whose pet he had treated, who owed him money, or where he bought supplies. He was back to square one.

Griffin searched everywhere for signs of fire until the smells from the previous fire began to make him sick. He went outside to get fresh air and find something for a headache from the truck when he saw a flicker of light on the roof. Griffin didn't hesitate to call the Fire Department, the dream had been an omen. When he made them aware, he began using a water hose to wet the roof. Tired from lack of sleep and nursing a sick headache, Griffin was in no shape to fight a fire alone.

By daybreak, he was completely drained. His head felt like it had been on fire. His sinus was full of smoke and he couldn't breathe well. He was forced to sit in the truck and watch the roof of his office caved in from the water. Water was destroying as much as the fire. The knowledge made Griffin weep in despair. All that was left of his business was the extension to the clinic where he had the kennels.

Fortunately, the animals were taken elsewhere. His associates made sure the pets were taken to another clinic out of town. A television station, reporting the news about the fire, announced periodically where the pet owners could find their animals. If these people hadn't helped, Griffin would have suffered more heartache because no living thing would have survived the smoke engulfing the property.

He drifted off to sleep inside his truck and was awakened by a soft hand stroking his face and hair. Before opening his eyes, he reached up and grabbed the hand thinking it was Odette's soothing his aching head and tortured heart, and was surprised to see that it wasn't Odette, but Lois whose hand he kissed.

"Hi there, sweetheart," Lois said.

"Why are you here, Lois?" Griffin demanded.

She replied, "I heard the news about another fire here at the clinic. I worried about you, so I drove by your apartment and your truck wasn't there. I took the chance to see if you were here. Is there anything I can do to help?"

Griffin didn't say a word, just scrambled out of his truck and walked over to the water hose. Drinking deeply from the flow of water, he was able to gather his thoughts before returning to Lois. He owed her an answer since he'd left confused standing next to his truck.

"Lois, I appreciate your concern, but there isn't anything you can do for me or my business," he stated.

"I can follow you home and make sure you have something to eat," she replied.

Griffin cleared his throat. Having Lois follow him home was the last thing he needed. He wanted Odette at his apartment, not her, so he quickly said, "Lois, I got married yesterday. By now, I should have a wife at home waiting for me."

"You what?" She yelled.

"I got married, yesterday. My wife should be at the apartment by now. I left her to check us out of the hotel, so I could check on this fire," he added.

At the top of her voice, Lois rambled, "what about all the compliments you gave me and our weekends at The Governor? Were you two-timing me? I thought you loved me! How can you be married? I saw your mother yesterday at the bank and she didn't say anything to me. Does she know? Is this witch at our hotel?"

The pain in Griffin's head was causing his stomach to lurch and Lois' ranting didn't help. Everything seemed to be crashing down on him. Instead of defending himself, he softly said, "I have to leave, Lois. I will explain everything to you one day. Just not this one."

Griffin stepped into his truck and closed the door. Then he drove away leaving Lois standing in the parking lot of his clinic still screaming at him. All he wanted was to lie in bed. He wanted to vanish and not think about anything, even Odette

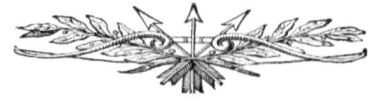

Zion, Jesus, and I watched Lois drive away, but we knew she was not leaving pacified by any means. We could hear her thoughts. She'd just left Griffin's apartment, so she knew the

wife wasn't there. She turned her car towards the Governor, sure that was where this woman would be. Lois was mortified, very angry, and wanting blood, so on the way to the hotel, she called the bank and took a sick day. She wanted more time to confront the woman who stole her man.

Zion demanded, are we allowing Lois to ruin their marriage? Or worse?"

Jesus calmly answered, "remember what Father said, nothing will destroy what He has planted. Sometimes the plantings get stepped on and appear to be hopelessly dead, but they still manage to break through the darkness and live."

Back in the hotel room, Odette was fully awake and grimacing in pain. When she threw back the covers and discovered why she hurt. Her knee was almost twice it's normal size. She should have used at least one crutch yesterday, it had been too soon to walk unassisted, even on her wedding day.

Realizing she was alone, she called out to Griffin, hoping he was in the bathroom. When he didn't answer, she hobbled to the door and knocked before entering. Still no Griffin. She found her crutches leaning against the wall next to the bathroom door and turned to grab one, that's when she noticed the note with her name written on it.

Dear Odette, I'm sorry for leaving you alone, but I couldn't sleep and had to check on the clinic. I called a cab to take me to the apartment, so I could get my truck. You have your car. When you are ready, you can check out of the room. Have the hotel staff help you with the luggage. Make yourself at home in the apartment. The address is 502 Applegate Drive, Apt. 2. Use your GPS to find it easily. See you soon. Love Griffin.

Hurt and disappointment crossed Odette's face. Reading her mind, we saw worry mixed in her heart as well. She wondered if the marriage was over before the honeymoon had even started.

She wanted to call Griffin, but quickly realized she didn't have his cell number. She couldn't do anything until she had her knee in check, but it was hard maneuvering with one crutch. She managed to find pain relievers in her luggage. Then she gathered ice cubes in a towel from the wet bar to place on her knee to reduce the swelling.

While she rested and waited for the pain meds to work, she turned on the television. The station was already on the local news and that's when she found out the clinic had caught on fire, again. There was no news of Griffin, but Firefighters had fought the blaze for several hours and pet owners were being alerted where their pets were taken.

All thoughts about her knee fled. Her heart was breaking for Griffin, the clinic was his pride and joy. He'd worked very hard to establish the business. "She was sure he needed her, and she wasn't there to console him. She couldn't even call him to let him know that she cared. After dressing quickly, she packed her bags, took another break then called the front desk for assistance with the luggage. She must go to the apartment and wait.

Lois went to the hotel's front desk and asked for the luxury suite. When the attendant said the couple hadn't completely checked out of the room, she knew she had the woman trapped. Her intent was nasty. She planned to unleash all her furies on this man-thief and give her a beating she wouldn't forget.

Jesus rushed to Zion's side, wrapped His arms around her and said in her ear, "this will be hard to watch. Would you like Father present?".

She didn't need to answer Jesus' question; our sweet Abba materialized and took her out of Jesus' arms. He wasn't allowing her to endure the unpleasant time alone. He wanted to soothe her emotions and showed her other lovely sights.

Jesus had made preparations before Odette ever opened the door to Lois. The whole bedroom was full of angels hidden in the background, there to pick up the pieces and help.

Odette heard the knock on the suite's door and quickly limped over to open it for the attendant. Instead of a man, Odette was greeted by a lady's fist to her face.

Falling hard to the floor, Odette screamed, "please don't hurt me! Take my bag. Just don't hurt me!"

"Witch, I'm not here for your money, I'm out for blood. You stole my man," Lois hollered back.

Odette countered as she rubbed her jaw. "what do you mean? I haven't stolen anyone's man."

"Griffin Waters is my fiancee. He doesn't love you! We've been seeing each other a very long time. You're just a gold-digger. How dare you come in and scoop him up for his fortune. You don't love him. You won't understand an Indian's needs," Lois spouted.

Struggling to stand on her feet, Odette moved away from the door and squared her shoulders to face Lois, "I don't have to answer to you. I suggest you leave before I scream for help. Someone will hear and call the police."

When Odette didn't want to fight, Lois saw red, rushed in and grabbed Odette's shirt, spitting out the first lie that entered her head hoping it would prompt a fight. "We'll see who wins him! I'm pregnant with his baby. He'll leave you for a true Indian heir, you white-trash slut."

Lois' words ripped through Odette's heart. Astonished, she jerked herself free from Lois' grip only to lose her balance, again. Odette didn't fall on the floor, she dove head first into a glass coffee table. Lois stared in shock, she didn't know what to do, Odette was unconscious, and her blood was pooling on the floor. Instead of trying to find help, Lois panicked and ran from the room thinking Odette was dead and she'd be responsible.

Jesus' angels were there to rescue Odette. They'd been ordered to whisper suggestions and guide people to help. The hotel attendant Odette had summoned to help pack her car was the first person on the scene. As the elevator door opened to Odette's floor, he noticed an Indian lady rushing from Odette's room. When he came to the opened door, he saw the unconscious Odette on the floor in a pool of blood. With fumbling fingers, he called 911 from the room's phone, then he called the front desk for extra help. Three other attendants rushed in and began treating Odette. Each one had an angel alongside them assisting and giving suggestions.

The attendants heeded every word that came to their mind. While they waited for Paramedics to arrive, two tended Odette's gashes, so she wouldn't bleed out. The first attendant found Odette's car fog inside her handbag packed luggage inside the jeep. Then he volunteered to follow the ambulance to the hospital in her vehicle when someone agreed to pick him up.

Every step was pre-ordained. Odette's things and her jeep were at the hospital when the ambulance arrived. All the attendant had to do was give the emergency room clerk her handbag. The items in it gave the hospital Odette's personal identification and insurance information.

Jesus had everything arranged and Odette was admitted without a hitch. Her insurance company was notified, and a nurse found contacts listed as Mom and Dad on Odette's cell phone and notified them. Odette's parents were on their way to Oklahoma.

The police researched the hotel records to find who had been renting the room. Griffin Waters' name was listed, so they contacted him. Griffin was informed that a lady in the room had been badly injured and taken to the hospital. They also said they expected foul play or possible homicide from what the hotel attendant said he'd witnessed.

The news shattered Griffin. He wanted to rush to Odette's side. His world was ending, and he couldn't wrap his head around the excessive information. In less than a week, he'd known bliss beyond compare followed by deep despair. He could rebuild his business, but what would he do if Odette died? All he could think was that he'd been a fool to leave her alone.

Griffin forgot about his headache. The threat of Odette's looming death almost choked him. An angel stationed close by helped him regain positive energy and his faith in medicine returned.

Instead of using positive energy correctly, he took the available power given him and changed it into anger. He focused that anger on Lois, sure she was the young lady the police suspected. He would make her pay.

Loose Ends and Suspicions

It was difficult watching Griffin mechanically go through angry motions, but even harder seeing Zion fret over Odette's broken body.

She cried softly for Abba to hear. "Odette, Odette, my sweet Odette, she is slowly losing life and a will to live"

Zion moaned and groaned until Abba relented, and showed her that Odette was in good care. Jesus had every detail established surrounding her and ready to assist with her treatment; including the right blood type, and medicine.

To calm Zion further, and make her feel useful, Abba said, "Zion, whisper empowering words into the atmosphere, give Jesus' angels some power from them. Your words are powerful. Angels thrive on words from us. Every word they hear you make will help them beat away the threats of death looming over Odette."

Zion perked-up at Abba's suggestion to help Odette. Speaking directly to the earth's atmosphere focusing good thoughts her way, Zion vehemently declared that the fear of death had no power because Jesus had the keys to death, hell, and the grave. Then, she spoke to Odette's flesh and commanded it to rise from the ashes. We watched the angels as if on cue, surround Odette and respond to Zion's words with thunderclaps and earsplitting praises.

Then we saw a visible change in Odette's body. Mechanical devices connected to her arm proved that her blood pressure was regaining strength. It also meant death had relinquished its hold on her life.

It was a pleasure seeing Zion smile again. It showed me something I would need to remind all the humans from now on; death hates hearing words of hope, love, and victory spoken aloud.

Anger fueled Griffin as he rushed to The Governor. He wanted to be with Odette, but the police demanded information about Lois. Upon arriving, he ran up the stairs instead of taking the elevator. Police were everywhere. When he went into the room, he understood why they demanded answers from him. A lot of Odette's blood was on the floor beside broken furniture. The sight made his knees buckle.

Griffin answered every question asked of him. He wanted Lois behind bars so he told the police where she lived, where she worked, and who her friends were. When the police finished their questions, he rushed to the hospital but was blocked, again.

His anger escalated when staff refused to give him information about Odette. Because he didn't have proof she was his wife, the only thing they were allowed to say was that a woman was in ICU, listed as Odette Payne, and under police protection.

Griffin pounded on the information desk and demanded to speak with someone in authority. An official politely said he had to produce a marriage certificate as proof or leave. He begged the gentleman to let him a phone call to the Magistrate

Court before he left, but he was blocked, again. This time, it was the Court Secretary who informed him the judge was on vacation until Sunday evening, and he could see him on Monday.

Griffin lost his temper and began shouting at the lady on the phone. Rather than take his verbal abuse she hung up the phone. Like a mad-man, Griffin began to swear at everyone, and the hospital authority called security to escort him out of the hospital. We watched his emotions fall apart in his truck.

"Do I need to speak a positive word in his direction?" Zion asked Abba.

"No, my dear. Griffin is in a dark place and angels don't want to be around him. Anger is the source of his strength, there are no positive energies working for him. We'll have to watch him go through mental hell before he comes to his senses and cries out for Jesus," Abba answered.

"There isn't anything we can do?" Zion inquired.

Abba relented, "your presence may help. He's used to Mother Nature's ways. You can use your earthy wiles to make him see the truth. Give him something to ponder."

"What do you mean, wiles of the earth?" Zion asked.

"He needs something to question. Then you can use your mental strength, instead of your words, to help him see the light. Focus your thoughts towards him as if he were stuck in a womb. Your mental energies may have to push him out into the open. Angels are ordered to help you. They are at your disposal. If they see you helping Griffin they will assist you. Just remember, Griffin needs a born-again experience to recoup all he's lost. Jesus has to be the one who catches the big baby." Abba said with a smile.

I could see that Griffin's mind was in total darkness. He didn't have a job to go too, a wife to hold, or anyone to talk with, so he drove to the liquor store. He'd wanted to escape his problems with booze. Purchasing three large bottles of rum, he left the store and drove home to self-medicate until he couldn't see, hear, or think while he waiting for the Judge's return.

Zion waited until Griffin was completely under the influence of the alcohol, and passed out on his couch before injecting herself into his mind. He greeted her when she entered his drug-induced sleep with a stupid looking sly smile on his face. Sarcastically he snarls, "there you are, where were you when I needed you most? Some god you are."

"Why didn't you call me, Griffin? I've been ready to help you," Zion asked him.

"Aren't you supposed to know all things? I just had my whole life destroyed and you didn't care. Why don't you kill me?" He blurted.

Zion thrust back angrily, "I don't want to kill you, Griffin! You're doing that all by yourself! I've come to help you!"

"Wave your magic wand and help. Then go away," he spits.

"Look at me, Griffin!" Zion shouts. "I'm leaving you two clues. Figure out what they mean, and you will know what to do. You know the answers. Odette explained them to you several nights ago in between your sexual romps."

"Okay, fine. Leave the clues. I need rest," Griffin spews.

Zion didn't say another word to Griffin. She places two small charms from Odette's bracelet on Griffin's couch and returned to Abba. She confessed, "I baited him. Now all I have do is bless him with my thoughts."

Griffin slept fourteen hours before fully waking. His wet trousers showed him why Randy always smelled like alcohol and urine.

He wanted coffee badly, so before going to the bathroom for a shower, Griffin stumbled into the kitchen and filled the coffee pot. He also swallowed a few aspirins for his aching head.

Once he'd showered, he dressed and returned the kitchen for coffee. His first cup didn't remove the cobwebs from his head, so he added a splash of rum to his brew. In minutes he felt better. *That's what hair of the dog means*, he thought to himself. Right after the thought, he felt ashamed of his actions. He'd promised himself and his dad years ago, that he would never succumb to alcohol. Their biological nature had a weakness to the drink and he didn't want turn out like Randy.

Griffin took his coffee back to the couch where he'd slept the night before. Before he sat, he rubbed his hands over the material to see if the couch was wet, and that's when he noticed two bracelet charms; a little anchor and a square with the word 'cornerstone' engraved in the middle of it.

He gulped down the cup of coffee and went to the kitchen for more of the same to help him think. Looking at the charms, he wondered where they had come from. Other than his mother, Odette was the only woman who ever allowed inside his apartment.

The thought of Odette sent his head reeling with pain, again. He wanted to be near her very badly. He fought back tears and went to the counter for more rum to put in his coffee. While pouring the rum into the cup, he looked out the kitchen window and noticed a beautiful swan swimming in the lake across the street. As if stung by a bee, Griffin remembered Zion's visit.

He stared at the charms in his hand, but he didn't know what clue Zion wanted him to remember. He just remembered Odette wearing a charm bracelet on their wedding day.

Griffin begged, "Mother Nature, please come back. I'm sorry for the insulting remarks I made last night. What do the charms mean? How are they going to help me?"

Hearing Griffin's plea made Zion smile. It proved the plan was working.

Everything Is Backward

Zion gave Griffin time to muddle through everything he and Odette had talked about since the day they met. Rather than watch his pain every single minute, she asked if she could focus on Odette for a little while.

Abba didn't mind. He wanted her involved in many issues, Odette and Griffin were just the trials run before moving her onto others. He asked her, "Zion, be honest with me; are you strong enough to help Jesus and Spirit?"

Her reply was sweet, "my body is extremely strong, but I can't say my mind and emotions are up to your standards. While focusing my strength on Griffin, I've come to realized it's my mental disabilities that have humanity in the mess they are in."

"Explain," Abba asked her.

"If we hadn't formed Adam to take on my physical attributes his spirit wouldn't have failed him. Fleshly needs make everything weak; including me. We'd all be trapped in a mental form of hell if it hadn't been for Jesus coming to our rescue. I appreciate Him, He is great, but He is not you. My flesh needs you with me at all times. Haven't we tested that fact enough?

"Then you won't have to be alone anymore. I can do all things from any place. I don't have to be sitting in heaven to make things cooperate smoothly and if I'm, to be honest with you, I love watching you and my Son work together. Field trips are stimulating," He shared.

Mechanical beeps stirred Odette enough to open her eyes. Seeing the monitors brought the memory of her falling into a glass table and passing out. She looked around for Griffin, but he wasn't there. So, when a nurse passed her room door, she cried out, "Miss, can you help me?"

"Hello, Ms. Payne. It's good to see you awake. You gave all of us a real scare," the nurse said.

"Why? Do I have internal injuries or something?" Odette asked.

"No, you lost a lot of blood before the ambulance came to your rescue. It took several pints of blood before you stabilized. You have a bad cut on your head, but a piece of glass punctured the brachial artery in your arm. You nearly bled out.

Take things slow. You have some bruising on your torso that will make breathing difficult and your knee is swollen," the nurse informed.

Odette explained, "Thanks for the update. I appreciate your help. I dislocated my knee several days ago. I had it splinted until the day before yesterday. Maybe I should keep it splinted."

The nurse nodded then made a note inside of Odette's chart. "Can I get you something to drink?" The nurse asked.

"I would like some water and something for pain, but I really need to know if my husband has been by," Odette said.

"No one has visited you Mrs. Payne, but we did contact your parents. They should be here soon," the nurse answered.

"My name is Odette Waters. My husband is Griffin Waters. are you sure he hasn't been around?" Odette probed.

"No one has visited or called. I can call him if you wish," the nurse offered.

Odette didn't have Griffin's number, but she knew the name of the clinic. "Call Waters Animal Clinic, I'm sure he is there."

The nurse looked at her with a stunned face, before answering, "the Clinic burned down recently. Don't you have another way to contact your husband?"

Odette answered, "no I don't." She remembered he didn't use a cell phone. He'd have to find her."

The nurse left to fetch Odette's water and to find out what to give her for pain. When she brought the requested items, she didn't hang around to talk. Odette was left alone and confused with only splinters of memory to focus her thoughts on. She tried to remember what happened.

Odette didn't know it, but the nurse called the Police Department before giving Odette the water and medication. The hospital had been ordered to call them the moment Ms. Payne was awake, so they could question her about the incident.

Odette was sitting upright surfing channels on the television when a police officer walked into her room and reached to shake her hand, "Good Morning, Ms. Payne. My name is Officer Albright. I need to ask you a few questions about what happened to you yesterday at the Governor Hotel. Can you accommodate me.?"

While extending her hand to the officer, Odette replied, "there's not much I can share, Officer Albright. I remember calling the front desk and asking to have an attendant help me pack my luggage in my car. When someone knocked on my door, I thought it was the help I'd called for. When I opened the door, I was struck in the face by a young Indian lady."

"Do you know this woman?" the Officer asked.

"I've never seen her before, but she let me know she was unhappy with me. She claimed I'd stolen her fiancee," Odette answered

"Did she push you into the table?" He asked.

"No, sir. I jerked out of her grasp and lost my balance. She was angry, but I didn't feel like she wanted to kill me," Odette confessed

"Just an angry rant, then?" The Office asked.

Odette smiled and said, "just a rant. A woman scorned."

The Officer smiled and said, "then I'll let you rest. We wanted to make sure you were safe."

"Thank you, Officer. I appreciate the concern," she replied.

When the Officer vacated the room, Odette lay her head back on the pillow and closed her eyes. The medicine she'd taken was making her sleepy. Drifting off to sleep, she relived every second before she fell, and worst of all, she watched her life fall apart in slow motion.

Griffin was engaged and expecting a baby with the Native American lady who attacked her. Placing herself in the lady's shoes, she couldn't blame her for being enraged. The lady was pregnant and thought she had a secure future.

Griffin never told Odette he was rich. She remembered his apartment, it sure didn't look fancy, in fact, it was sparse and unkempt, some would think he was almost homeless.

What hit Odette hard during her sleepy state of mind, was that Griffin had totally abandoned her. She almost died. He hadn't even called. Odette couldn't help but wonder if he was making up with that lady.

Odette's anger flared. She had been happy before meeting him. She never intended to find a man on her vacation. All she wanted to do was research Indigenous culture. She fretted over what she had done. She wanted to do the right thing. Now there was a baby involved. All the facts were screaming at her. If Griffin really cared, he'd be by her side. She would apply for an annulment and end his problem.

A noise jarred her from the thoughts. When she opened her eyes, standing beside her bed were her Mom and Dad. With tears spilling onto her cheeks, she said to them, "You came! Take me home. I want to go home."

Mrs. Payne gave Odette a kiss on the forehead and said, "we plan to, dear. We flew in on the earliest fight we could find, so we could bring you home. We rented a car at the airport and drove directly to this hospital.

The head nurse said you were doing great and would be released to a regular room soon. Dad and I are hoping the doctor may release you to our care instead. We will beg him if we have too."

We had strict orders from Abba not to intervene. It didn't surprise us when the doctor agreed with her parents and released Odette to their care. His only instruction was to make her eat and get some more rest.

Zion protested, but her arguments were ignored. Abba wouldn't budge. He was allowing Odette to leave Oklahoma with her parents.

Zion argued with Him while Mr. Payne helped Odette into her jeep and gave the keys to Mrs. Payne. She finally gave up her arguments when Mr. Payne returned the rental car and they began the drive home to Georgia.

Tormented Souls

Once Odette was on the road home, Abba turned His attention to Zion. "You have to trust the process, Zion. I've watched the same scenario play out over-and-over. Don't you remember how the Israelites roamed around the same mountain for forty years, and how they murmured and complained the whole time?"

"What are you saying? Will Odette be forty years older before she and Griffin re-connect? I know what separation from you feels like. It's awful! I don't want that for her or Griffin." Zion protested with a pout.

Abba took Zion in His arms and said, "it won't be very long before we have them together again. At this present time, they are both in a very dark place, angry and wanting answers. They won't turn to us immediately, they will seek information from their family, friends, and religious upbringings. Jesus has to make sure they understand their answers don't come from outside forces, rules, and regulations, they only come from a relationship with Him."

"But we made ourselves known to them. We had one-on-one conversations, so why wouldn't they call on us?" Zion asked.

Abba burst into laughter. "They've forgotten all of that. Their thoughts have turned inward. They can't see us now. Once they see that family and friends don't have the answers, their minds will crave peace. We must wait.

Odette's family will point her to a church counselor and the Bible. The do's and don'ts found in the scriptures don't apply to this situation.

Griffin's mother will continue to shove her beliefs at him. When he refuses, she will give him more peyote and tell him to return to the woods and seek you. The clues you gave him will not help until he has time to be alone in peace. When he realizes that Jesus is there to help, he will obtain the strength to search for Odette.

Does this explanation help you understand the necessary process? Without relationships with us, they will never know peace and love the right way. We have to make sure they don't depend on people or religion anymore."

"Then I'm no longer angry with you. I admit my judgment was flawed. Help my unbelief. Never, ever leave me alone to my own devices or emotions," Zion responded.

Pacing the floor, and rubbing the charms between his fingers, Griffin tried to make sense of everything. He knew Friday would be a long day without seeing Odette and he worried about what she must be thinking.

A knock on his front door jolted him from the worried thoughts. When he opened the door, it was Officer Albright, who had come to inform him of Odette's decision.

Griffin threw the door back and motioned for Officer Albright to enter. He was very eager to hear any news of Odette's well-being. "How's Odette?" Griffin asked.

Officer Albright answered, "she was alert enough to answer my questions. I don't know her diagnosis, but I did see bandages on her forehead and arm."

"What did she tell you about the conflict?" Griffin asked.

"Only that it was a misunderstanding. Something about her stealing you from the other lady. I came to tell you that Ms. Payne did not press any charges against Lois Jones and inform you that the hotel management expects you to pay for the damages to the room." Albright shared.

"I'll take care of the damages. Did Odette ask questions about me?" Griffin probed.

"No, sir. I'm sorry." Office Albright said sympathetically. Then he left Griffin's apartment.

Griffin shut the door after Officer Albright, and another knock came on his door. It was his mother. "Why were the police here, Griffin? Are you holding Randy responsible for the fire? I'm the one who you should be angry with, Randy only did it for me."

"Mom, stop! Come in, sit down, take a breath, and talk slower. I have a headache," Griffin demands.

Irene found a seat on Griffin's sofa and noticed the empty rum bottle on the table in front of her. "I see why your head hurts, son. Where's Odette, is she drunk too?"

At that verbal jab, Griffin lost his temper and threw his coffee mug against a wall. "No, Mom! Odette is in the hospital because Lois tried to kill her yesterday."

Irene went white from Griffin's raging reaction to her statement. She almost hesitated to ask but needed to know what happened. Lowering her voice she asked softly, "Son, is Odette okay? What happened?"

Griffin was crying by this time from mental torture, so he shouted, "Do you really care? You made it very clear to us that you hate her. You didn't give her a chance to show you that she is a lovely person, intelligent, and well established.

I'm frustrated because the hospital won't allow me to see her. I don't know how she is. I must prove to the hospital authorities that she is my wife before can see her or have any information given to me. And as my luck would have it, the Magistrate Judge is out of his office until Monday and his secretary wouldn't help me; said she didn't have the authority. I am about to lose my mind."

"Let's change the subject, son. Why were the police here?" Irene asked him.

Griffin calmed down a bit, sat in the chair next to her and took a deep breath. "The officer came to tell me that he visited Odette in the hospital. He wanted to tell me that she wasn't filing charges against Lois and that I had to pay for the damages done the hotel room. When I asked him about Odette's health, he said she was alert and had several bandages on her body. That's all he offered.

He wasn't here to ask me if I wanted to file charges against Randy. I'm still debating on what to do about him. He's a grown man, Mom, and should be held accountable for his actions. You may have given him an idea, but you didn't throw the Molotov cocktail into my clinic office. People were inside the building as well as many pets, they could have been killed."

Irene was somewhat pacified by Griffin's answers, but she really wanted to escape more wrathful actions or judgmental remarks, so she sweetly said before leaving, "I'm sorry, son. I can see you wish to be alone to think over your issues. Call if you need me."

Griffin let her leave without escorting her to the door. When he heard the door close, he threw his body onto the couch, cracked open another bottle of rum, and drank straight from the bottle as he sobbed.

Three hours into to their drive home, Odette was also crying in the back seat of the jeep. When her mother asked why all the tears, her reply was that she was hurting and needed to relax somewhere.

Sharing a room with her parents made Odette feel like a child again. It intensified her low self-esteem even further. To escape reality she took a heavy dose of pain medicine, so she could fall asleep quickly.

Dreams of her nights with Griffin plagued her weary mind. Seeing his naked body over and over in the dreams only gave her a sexually frustrating night. Her dreams were so intense, her mother shook her awake to see if she was having a seizure.

Odette was embarrassed and didn't go back to sleep after that, she forced herself to stay awake by counting how many times her father fluttered his lips when he snored. She refused to entertain the thoughts of Lois and Griffin's baby. She was determined to do the right thing; the baby didn't ask to be conceived.

Instead of calling on Jesus for answers, she placed the blame on God, thinking He must have wanted Griffin with Lois instead of her. She recalled her Sunday School classes that always suggested people heed the flow, watch for signs of God's hand moving and then do the right thing. In this instance, she deduced that this baby was God's plan and she needed to back away. The child needed a relationship with Griffin.

When daybreak came, Odette hobbled to the bathroom before her parents awakened. Inside the small room, even toilets and tub reminded her of Griffin. Sponge-bathing at the bathroom sink, she complained softly about her reflection in the mirror, "why did you do this to me, Jesus? Why did you bring me all this way to get my head bashed in and have my heart crushed? I thought you were a God of love, you even said Griffin and I were meant to be. I wanted to love, but not at the cost of breaking up a family."

After hearing Odette say those things, Abba turned to Zion and said, "I told you she wouldn't remember the good visits but would blame us for all of her problems."

Confessions

Waking up in the same shape he had the day before, Griffin remembered to put a splash of rum in his coffee to ease his aching head. He didn't like the way he felt. His fuzzy head didn't ease until he forced himself to eat and take a hot shower.

He needed fresh air to completely recover, so, after two more cups of coffee without the rum added, Griffin managed to dress and leave his apartment. If he couldn't be with Odette, there was only one other thing that could drive him outside, and that was the need to find Lois and hear what she had to say.

Grifin wanted to confront Lois in public. He didn't want to lose his temper and being around others would help him stay in check. When Lois wasn't at work, he had no choice but to go to her apartment.

On the drive over, he asked himself what he wished to accomplish by seeing Lois. What did he want to hear? Did he want to hear Lois' side of the story or to hear what really happened to Odette?

Lois was at home and she opened the door to him. The first words she said were, "I've been expecting you. The police have thoroughly questioned me, so I'm prepared for your interrogation. What do you want to know? Do you even care about my side of the story?"

Griffin truthfully answered, "I don't know either side. The hospital won't allow me to see Odette. All I have are statements from the police. Tell me the truth, Lois. That's all that matters to me."

"Come in and have a seat. It may take a while for me to gather my courage to tell you everything, but I need to do it. I feel awful about what happened to your wife. I didn't intend for her to get hurt. I only wanted to make her feel threatened," Lois admitted.

Griffin didn't want to get too comfortable, so he went to the kitchen table and found a chair. Once Lois sat across from him he asked, "will you tell me everything? I must have hurt you deeply, but I never promised you anything more than a friendship with sexual pleasures. You know this is the truth."

"A girl can hope, Griffin! I love you and I thought I showed how much I care. I held nothing back, but the words. I hoped.in time you would need me more than just for sex. When you told me so bluntly, that you had married, I went insane," Lois answered.

"What happened after I left you Thursday morning? I had to leave. When you began to scream at me, my head almost burst. I was already sick from smoke inhalation.and couldn't take any more agitations. I didn't mean to hurt you, Lois. You caught me at a stressful time and I felt it fair to tell you the truth and not make you assume I needed your help," Griffin stated honestly.

Lois bit her lip. Then she stood and asked, "can I have your word that you won't get mad?"

"I can't promise that, Lois! You attacked my wife, but I will promise not to lash out at you. I may say words I'll regret later, but I will not harm you," He answered.

Satisfied with Griffin's answer, Lois took a huge breath and said, "after you left me in the clinic parking lot, I remembered there wasn't a car parked at your apartment. I took a chance that this woman was still at The Governor and drove over. When I asked the desk clerk about the room, he said the room wasn't available because the current occupants hadn't left.

I knew I had her trapped. I knocked on the door and when she opened it, I punched her in the face."

Lois stepped behind the kitchen counter after saying that and didn't say anything else until she was sure Griffin was holding his temper in check. She could see the struggle on his face, but he was staying still and being quiet.

"Would you like something to drink, Griffin?" Lois asked as she gathered the courage to continue.

"No thanks. Continue telling me everything," He said.

Lois stayed behind the counter and opened a can drink for herself. "I didn't know she had a bad leg until she struggled to regain her composure, but that didn't stop me from attacking her with my words. When she didn't fight back, I grabbed her by the shirt and said something stupid."

"What did you say, Lois?" Griffin demanded.

"I told her I was pregnant, and you'd prefer having an Indian family. That's when she wrenched herself free from me and fell into the table. She was unconscious, and blood was pouring on the floor. I panicked! I thought she was dead, so I ran." Lois blurted.

Griffin slammed his fists on the kitchen table and stood. "Be glad she didn't hold the attack against you, Lois!. I wouldn't have been merciful if she'd died." Griffin shouted before storming out of Lois' apartment.

After leaving Lois, Griffin drove quickly to the hospital, but he didn't go inside. He'd been ordered not to return unless he had proof of marriage or security would usher him out, again. So, he sat in the parking lot and talked to the sky. "Odette, I love you so much. I'm dying inside without you. If only we could talk. I'd straighten out this mess. What must you think of me?

I spoke with Mother Nature. She gave me some of your jewelry and told me to make sense of the pieces. I haven't a clue as to what these charms mean. I just know they are from your bracelet. I wish I could remember. Don't give up on me. I'll come running on Monday."

Odette and her parents were hundreds of miles away from Oklahoma when Mrs. Payne finally approached Odette with questions. Like most mothers, she had to know what happened to her daughter. Odette had always been a level-headed person and hearing that she had been attacked by another person upset her greatly.

"Odette, you know we have to hear what happened to you. Do you want to tell us? Dad and I were frantic until we saw you again." Mrs. Payne asks.

The last thing Odette wanted to talk about was what happened and why, but she owed the truth to her parents even if it was humiliating. "I understand Mom. I owe the two of you an explanation. Promise not to think badly of me," Odette asks.

"We won't, honey. Everyone goes through hard times. We just don't like them happening to you, so if we can help you get through them we will," her mother warmly explained.

"Well, you know I traveled West to research more of the Indigenous culture, especially about the Creek Indians. I did something extremely out of character for me. I met a lovely Indian man, named Griffin Waters and we instantly fell in love. Crazy in love, and in a few days, we married," Odette struggled to say.

"You did what?" Mr. Payne asked, in shock!

Odette confessed, "I got married, Dad. Then on the same day of my marriage, Griffin's business was set on fire by a drunk relative. While he was away from me taking care of those details, his old girlfriend showed up at the hotel and began to threaten me."

"Did she mean to kill you?" Her Mom asked.

"No, she only wanted to scare me. She said I had a battle on my hands to keep Griffin because she was pregnant, and he'd prefer a family within his own race. I turned away from her too quickly and fell into a glass table. She didn't push me," Odette shares.

Hearing that Odette had fallen in love with an Indigenous man, pricked her mother's heart. The news uncovered a hidden grief she'd kept secret and never talked to Odette about. The memory of what happened to her own mother, before giving birth to her, forced her to ask this question. "Why do you want to leave him, honey?"

Odette wiped tears from her face and answered, "Griffin never called or visited me at the hospital. I was there almost two days. It made me realized I had been a fool to marry him. I'm sure he ran back that the other woman. I'm determined to do the right thing for his baby regardless of my feelings. My plan is to file for an annulment and set him free."

Mrs. Payne assured Odette they wouldn't ask her anything else, but as Odette spoke the words, Mrs. Payne was concerned for her daughter's mental well-being. History had a way of repeating itself and she feared the worst for her daughter.

The next time Mrs. Payne was alone with her husband she explained her fears to him. They didn't want Odette to be sad, so they agreed to console her as much as they could but planned to point her toward their church counselor when arriving home. Odette would have to muddle through this issue alone until then, they agreed to stay out of her way and not share their opinions. Plus, it wasn't the time to reveal a secret Mrs. Payne harbored, because it would change Odette's life.

Living Hell

Sunday morning, Griffin decided to spend the day rummaging through the ruins of his business just to make time pass instead of drinking himself into a stupor. Before leaving his apartment, he called one of his associates who is a computer whiz to ask if there was any hope of salvaging the information on his computers.

Griffin rushed to the clinic after hearing there may be hope of gathering information from something called 'the cloud. Scavengers were on the site. when he arrived A couple of drug addicts were probing through what use to be his medicine cabinets.

Griffin pulled a rifle out of his truck and shouted from a distance, "hey, you two are trespassing. I'll shoot you if you don't leave. Wait! Clean your pockets of my things before you do. I know you found some meds."

When the men emptied their pockets and ran, Griffin went to where the items lie on the ground. The medications they tried to steal would have harmed them if taken. It grieved him to think that drug addicts usually didn't differentiate what could and couldn't be consumed by humans, they only wanted to get high or have something to sell to others more dependent on drugs than themselves.

Worried they may return and try to harm him, Griffin called the Police Department to report the incident and was told to wait in his truck until a police officer arrived. The minutes he waited seemed like hours and only gave Griffin more time to think about Odette. He was sick without her and realized she was his drug of choice and he needed her badly. He craved her scent, the smoothness of her porcelain skin and the way she shook from

141

his touches. She'd ignited a desire in him that she could only quench and he never wanted to be free from the influence.

A knock on the truck's window broke Griffin's thoughts and he looked up to find a police officer ready to take notes and complaints. The rest of the day, he and the police officer looked through the rubble gathering drugs and paraphernalia, so the thieves wouldn't have substances on the streets. The work was tedious and he almost forgot why he came to the clinic.

Griffin was very tired and felt he did a good deed by removing the drugs from his property. He was also grateful to have precious information inside the melted computers. That night, he relaxed a bit without the aid of alcohol. A few more hours and he could go to the Magistrate Judge's Office and get the papers allowing him to see Odette.

Zion was shaking again. We all knew she was having trouble knowing what Griffin was about to face. Abba wrapped her in His arms again before saying, "you know Griffin has a point. There is nothing like having your woman tremble at your touch. Especially if it is for the right reasons"

"What do you mean," she asked.

"You don't need to shake. Griffin will get through this birthing process. Try and relax, his world hasn't turned completely upside down, yet," Abba explained.

"I'm doing the best I can. Watching this brings back painful memories of when I was trapped as Satan's slave. Watching Griffin get his hopes up makes me sad. I can't create positive energy by watching him struggle. I'm making things worse. My body and mind are not agreeing with each other. I can think positive, but my body wants to react to his scared emotions. I'm trying to help, but it may take decades to calm Griffin down if you leave everything up to me," she shares.

"I'm here to help. I have all the time in the world, my dear. Covering for you is a joy for me. There'll always be times when I must make adjustments or tip things back into balance. Don't quit. You are helping me. Fight to stay positive, forget the past, and believe in my love for you and everything will work out," He assures her.

"I promised to do the best I can. I already know what will take place. Life moves slower in the earthly realm and I'll just be patient and try not to rush Griffin. It really helps to have you here. I relax around you."

Smiling, she gazes into Abba's eyes and lowered her voice seductively, "I have an idea. Since your plans for Griffin are set, and tomorrow is the day he will flip over, why don't you keep my thoughts focused on you instead of the contractions Griffin must endure.

I must not be allowed to focus on my past. Griffin's born-again experience is too important. Let's leave the guys to watch over him, so I will tremble the way you like. I need backrubs, and foot massages from you, I may even return the favor."

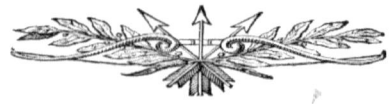

At 6:00 a.m. in the morning, Griffin's cell phone woke him up. His mother was calling, and he answered quickly. "Hi, Mom. Why are you calling so early? Are you okay?"

"I'm fine, son. I'm calling for Lucy. She's scared to ask you if she still has a job. I know you have plans for today, but you also have other responsibilities to deal with. Make those calls, Lucy probably isn't the only one wondering," Irene said.

Griffin moaned, and rugged sleep out of his eyes, "Thanks for calling, Mom. It hadn't crossed my mind that Lucy and my associates may be worried. I'll handle it right away."

"What are you going to say?" She asked.

"There is no job to go to, Mom. I have to terminate my employees so, they can file for unemployment. I hope they will want to return when I have the clinic rebuilt, but that may take several months, and they'll need money soon," he answers.

"I understand. I'll let you get to it then. Have a good day, son," she said before ending the call.

Griffin spent most of the morning dealing with employee issues, insurance adjustors, and police who wanted his decision on what to do about Randy. By 2:00 in the afternoon, he finally managed to get to the Magistrate Judge's Office only to be told the Judge wouldn't be back until the next day. When the secretary tried to explain, Griffin screamed 'don't bother' and hastily left the courthouse.

That evening, Griffin's mother paid him another visit and found her son on the way to being drunk again. By his appearance, she instantly concluded he hadn't seen Odette. "Griffin, has it occurred to you that you may have upset Mother Nature? Your life has been one mess after another."

Instead of getting angry with his mother, Griffin regained enough focus and answered without sarcasm. He wanted her to leave feeling she had made a point, so she wouldn't stay and argue with him, "no, Mom. I hadn't thought that. What do you suggest?"

"Do you still have the peyote I gave you? It will help you commune with her a lot easier than the booze your drinking," she answered.

"I still have some of it. I'll take your advice only if you leave me alone," he offered.

"Sure, son. Call me soon, okay." She agreed and left his apartment.

As soon as the door closed, Griffin turned off his cell phone and took his bottle of rum to the bedroom. His only plans for the evening were to watch a ball game on his television and drink until he fell asleep in bed. He needed the distractions to numb his mind, so he wouldn't think about Odette, go strangle his mother, or kill Lois. All he had inside of him was rage and the rage wasn't solving anything.

The Controlling Spirit

Jesus and I were happy when Abba and Zion left us alone with Griffin. This way we could work with him and not worry about frustrating Zion or making her uncomfortable. Griffin had to be saved from himself and forced into submission.

Ever since his father's death, a raging spirit has driven Griffin. He lost his opportunity to find his way in a loving environment when his mother started worrying about how they would make ends meet. Her emotions forced his life into one struggle after the next to survive.

We knew today would be our only chance to get our point across to him. Jesus commanded His angels to prepare the way. Their first order was to flush out the spirit controlling Griffin's soul.

The alarm clock began to beep at 7:00 a.m. and continued to beep until Griffin slammed his fist on top of the button. Groaning from a headache, he managed to crawl out of bed and stumbled into his kitchen for coffee that wouldn't be immediately available. He'd forgotten to prepare the coffee maker the night before.

Swearing at the top of his lungs, he quickly put coffee grounds in the coffee maker and turned it on, then went to shower as the coffee brewed.

He refused to think about the day or get his hopes up like he had before. Instead, he enjoyed the hot water as it washes over his body until it ran cold. After drying and putting on deodorant, he changed into clean clothes and returned to the kitchen for his coffee.

Not wanting to appear drunk at the Magistrate Judge's Office or at the hospital, he added a small splash of rum to the coffee to beat down his hangover and drank it quickly. He poured his next cup of coffee into a travel mug, forced a piece of bread and slice of cheese down his throat and left his apartment.

Griffin's heart began to race when he parked his truck in the courthouse parking lot. Trying not to get too excited, he talked down to himself instead of being upbeat and the angels overheard him say, "nothing has ever been easy for me. If I don't get my marriage certificate today, I'll force someone to help me. I shouldn't have to wait like this, I have rights." The angels wanted to leave, but Zion's energy and Jesus' order forced them to stay.

His words revealed the controlling spirit. Rage was Griffin's evil master and causing him to have an impatient nature. It was giving him negative energy to be an insulting bully, but we were not allowing it to cause havoc to others today.

Inside the courthouse, angels worked around Magistrate Judge, Arnold Ponder, as he signed papers. They planned to use him to humble Griffin and make him feel ashamed of his actions. The Judge's intent was to have his secretary give Griffin the marriage certificate that day. He wasn't feeling well and wanted to go home. The only reason he came into the office was to handle the necessary issues; one of them being Griffin's.

Griffin walked into the office with his bullying rage already engaged and he began to demand his rights. That's when

Judge Ponder was prompted by an angel to take care of his secretary and not allow her to be threatened. As bad as he felt, he exited his office and went to face Griffin. "What's going on here, Mr. Waters? My secretary is not your enemy. I have your certificate ready here in my hand. There is no need to scream at us."

The angel's prompt worked. A wide-eyed Griffin stared at the beat up, Judge who was using crutches to enter the secretary's office in her defense. Humbled, Griffin said, "I apologize. I really need the certificate. My wife is in the hospital and I'm not allowed in the ICU unless I produce it."

"I'm sorry to hear about your wife, Mr. Waters. I understand your stress, but as you can see by my appearance, I was in an accident over the weekend. I would have been here yesterday to help you, but I had to have someone come to my rescue and bring me home," Judge Ponder explained.

Griffin was at a loss for words and highly embarrassed for his actions, so he thanks the Judge and leaves.

We knew Rage wasn't finished. It would use Griffin again soon. This time we planned to allow the rage to ignite but not blaze. Griffin had to see he wouldn't have anywhere or anyone to release the rage onto. To help him through this process, Jesus assigned one angel to follow Griffin. He was to lead Griffin along the right paths toward us. Once Griffin found out Odette had left town, we had him alone to ourselves, and Jesus would make sure the war inside of Griffin would end.

The speed limit didn't matter to Griffin. He broke every rule to get to the hospital. When he went inside the building, he noticed a gift shop that had flowers and thought it would be a lovely idea to grab some roses as a peace offering to give to his wife.

With flowers in hand, he went to the front desk and presented the necessary papers to the lady at the counter. When she couldn't find anyone with the last name of Payne listed, Griffin began to shake with fear. He almost fainted from his thoughts. *Had she died? Was she in a morgue?*

On cue, one of the angels had the nurse who treated Odette in Griffin's vicinity. When she overheard Griffin ask about Odette, she turned to listen to the conversation and noticed his expression when the clerk said Odette wasn't there. She rushed to Griffin's side and gently tapped him on the shoulder. "Mr. Waters, I can tell you about your wife. Follow me, please," she said.

"What, about Odette?" He asked.

"I'm the nurse who took care of Ms. Payne. She said she had a husband and wanted to know if you were visiting. I didn't know what to say to her. We had no information about you and we were instructed to call her parents as soon as she was admitted to our unit. They arrived late Friday afternoon and convinced the doctors to let them take Ms. Payne back home to Georgia. I'm sorry you weren't notified," she admitted.

Griffin shallowed hard and tried to hold his temper in check, "How was she? Did they take her home by ambulance?"

The nurse answered, "she gave us a scare at first, but after a few pints of blood and antibiotics, she revived quickly we planned to move her out of ICU and into a private room that evening. She has a nasty cut on her head and a punctured artery in her arm, but she is fine otherwise. She told me she'd hurt her knee a few days earlier. When I told her mother, we were planning to move her into a room, she asked the doctor if they could take her home instead. Odette was released a few hours after they arrived. You should find her at their home. They had

149

orders to make her rest. I need to return to work, now. Nice to meet you, Mr. Waters."

Before the nurse walked away, Griffin stopped her and handed her the vase of roses and said, thank you for coming to my rescue and telling me everything you knew. You deserve these." Then he walked out of the hospital deflated and Rage fed on his painful sobs.

It was time the angel confronted Rage for the first time. So, when Griffin kicked the tire of his truck to relieve some of the pent-up anger, the angel said, "why are you allowing Rage to hurt you?"

The spirit didn't reply to the angel. It wanted full control of Griffin, so it could continue to grow. Pity was Rage's food of choice and he had Griffin wrapped up in it and feeling sorry for himself. He didn't care about the pain in his foot or a voice in his head trying to change the mood.

Rage's prompts kept baiting Griffin. The ugly spirit made him blame Mother Nature for introducing him to Odette and then taking her from him. It was also urged him to seek her out and wage war. Even if meant suffering from the effects of peyote.

The peyote wasn't hard to find. The leftovers were still in his backpack from the time before. Snatching up the pack, Griffin's eyes fell on Odette's charms, but Rage used them also to remind Griffin Mother Nature had left him in a lurch and was cruel and destructive.

Griffin's thoughts angered the angel assigned to him enough for a retort. Instead of confronting Rage, the angel spoke to Griffin. "You don't know what cruel is. Try saying our mother is mean one more time."

"Who are you, and why are you tormenting me?" Griffin shouted.

"You'll know soon enough," the angel replied.

Griffin brushed off the threat and left the apartment. He was ready for a fight. On his way to the cabin in the woods, he kept feeding the anger with wicked thoughts. We had Rage right where we wanted and by the time he arrived at the cabin, it was looming large; inside of Griffin, on him, and around him. A large target to destroy.

Wrestling With Rage

Griffin didn't linger inside the small cabin. He grabbed the peyote and charms and ran to the woods where Mother Nature previously had revealed herself. We were prepared for the encounter and had the angel ready for the fight. Rage had a chain around Griffin's throat leading him around like a dog and we knew it wouldn't let go of him easily. If we were to succeed, Griffin would have to fight something besides Zion. He needed to see the truth for himself, so the angel morphed into Griffin's twin.

Griffin sat on the ground and leaned against the same tree as before, he threw the peyote pod in his mouth and began to chew. The same rush filled his body and things began to spin. The urge to vomit was instantaneous and after emptying his stomach of his meager breakfast, Griffin raised his head and was face to face with himself.

"What the hell!" Griffin screeched.

The angel answered, "were you expecting a woman to fight you?"

Griffin rubbed his eyes and wiped his mouth. He wanted to stand but was too dizzy. Instead, he spat, "are you Mother Nature trying to be funny?"

"No, but I've come in her place," the angel said.

"I demand her attention! She's the one who took my life away," Griffin yelled.

The angel baited, "you don't look dead to me. In fact, you are full of energy and I plan to deplete it."

Griffin managed to get to his feet and lunged at the angel with a small tree limb he picked up, "I'm not talking with you. Leave or I'll pummel you with this stick."

The angel snatched the limb from Griffin's grasp and slapped him on the back with it, "it's going to take more than this to hurt me."

The slap infuriated Griffin. With a loud scream, he slammed his body into the angel's belly. The angel didn't move but Griffin buckled and slid down the angel's body as if he'd hit a brick wall.

"Get up from the ground, and talk with me like a human being, instead of acting like a rabid animal," the angel demanded.

Griffin grabbed the angel by the pant leg and hissed, "not until I rip my face off your head. I didn't come here to argue with myself. My beef is with Mother Nature."

Instead of falling over as Griffin intended, the angel lifted Griffin off the ground with his leg. Once Griffin was placed on his feet, the angel said, "face me or you'll never see Mother Nature again."

"Who are you?" Griffin yelled.

Countering the angel replied, "I am an angel, sent to set you free."

"Free from what? I'm not a slave to anything. I have no rules placed on me," Griffin sneered.

The angel sighed, then said, "you are a fool. You are not acting like an adult with rational thinking. Come clean with yourself. Adjust your thoughts and get naked with the truth, so you can't fight what you must face.'

Still, under the drug's influence, and full of self-pity, Griffin began to undress. After taking everything off his body, he stood naked in front of the angel and said, "Now what? I'm bare as the day I was born. If I'm a fool I might as well look like one when I fight you."

The angel didn't laugh but wanted to. Instead, he took the opportunity to guide Griffin rather than angering him further. "Why don't you take a deep breath and focus on what I said while I destroy the raging spirit forcing you to do stupid things. Release your mind from the rage inside of you and give it to me. Then try and remember what information you were given in this place the last time you were here."

The angel's words worked. Something in Griffin snapped and with both hands, he grabbed his hair, fell to his knees, and shouted, "I'm tired of being angry all the time. Please help me."

The words forced Rage's chains from Griffin's neck and the evil spirit had to leave his mind, its hold on Griffin's soul was non-existent and it had to face the waiting angel. Rage's death was explosive, and the noise spread throughout the heaven and earth's atmosphere causing birds to fly and stir up a breeze. The sounds they made seemed like a cry for help and grabbed Griffin's attention that's when he saw a wolf and a swan again and instantly thought of Odette.

Instead of remembering who his spirit guide was, Griffin ran to the open crevasse on unsteady legs hoping to see Odette. Disgusted by Griffin's refusal to remember Jesus, the angel said, "the beast didn't lead you to Odette?"

Griffin didn't answer the angel but searched for his beloved. The site was the same as before. The little shelter still stood but there was no Odette. The naked and severely humbled Griffin crawled inside of it and submitted to Jesus. "Jesus, if you are really my spirit guide, I need you. I'm lost and can't find my way."

Born Again

Zion heard Griffin cry out for Jesus' help. "He's here! Griffin is now part of our family," she exclaimed to Abba.

"I told you Jesus would make sure he would come into our kingdom. I'm happy you didn't want to watch the process. Look at him now, he's naked as a newborn and ready for his milk." Abba informed her.

"Does this mean I can assist in his training?" Zion asked.

Abba answered, "your time will come soon. First, Jesus must help him find Odette. When that happens, you can help train both of them. You gave Griffin clues, let's wait until he figures out what they mean. Jesus' faithfulness must be planted firmly in his heart. Without total trust in Him, Griffin's life will flounder, and we can't allow that to happen."

Griffin was rocking from side to side when a bright light began to penetrate through the logs of the shelter. The brilliance grabbed his attention and forced him to look outside and into the face of Jesus, who was standing near the stream's edge.

Slowly, Griffin approached the Lord. When he was close, he knelt on one knee and said softly, "Jesus, please help me. I can't live this way any longer."

Jesus stepped closer to Griffin and took him by the shoulders, "Stand with both of your feet on the Holy ground,

Griffin. You have been born into God's kingdom of love and acceptance. Reconnect with everything around you and draw from love's flow. I'm with you now. Count on me always."

"I want to count on you. Help me find peace in my life again. I thought I had it with Odette," Griffin said.

Jesus smiled at Griffin and answered him sweetly, "I came at Odette's beckoning. She and I have a relationship you were just there to experience what we shared. Now that you've asked for me specifically, I promise to be with you too."

"I have so many questions," Griffin exclaims.

"I know you do. We'll take things slow, but wouldn't you like to have clothes on before we start our new journey together. Without a fire, mosquitoes will find your naked flesh and you'll be fighting them. I'd much rather have all your attention," Jesus joked trying to lighten the mood.

The two of them went back to where Griffin shed his clothes then they walked together back to the cabin. When they were inside the small house, Griffin said, "my problems started way before I met Odette, didn't they?"

"Yes, they did. Do you remember the first day you felt alone and scared? That's when you began to struggle against me. Remember what Zion told you? You weren't created to carry your parent's burdens. Your strong belief in native traditions forced, you to compromise and I couldn't help you. Not even your belief in Zion helped you feel loved the same way after your father died.

When he died, the loving environment you were born into vanished like a puff of smoke. Your mother wasn't in any shape after his death to keep the feelings of that love alive for you to grow into a strong man without fear. She's not at fault. Human love is fragile, but God's love is not. Share my life and grow up in His love for you. This way, you can thrive the way we want and not be controlled by an angry spirit any longer," Jesus suggested.

"I don't remember what it feels like not to harbor anger inside my mind. Anger was the driving force that made me who I am," Griffin said.

With a sad face, Jesus asked, "and where did anger drag you? What do you have left from all your hard work? Where is the love we gave you?"

"I understand," Griffin admits.

Jesus extends His arms and begins to look around, "Griffin, it's time to let love control your actions. Look around you. This loving world we're in is waiting to help you. Trust and patience in me. The Holy Spirit and I will help you find your way, you'll find it easier than fighting against a brick wall?"

Griffin snickered, "I butted heads with a brick wall a few minutes ago, he wasn't fun to come against."

"None of my avenging angels are fun. They are completely loyal to me and find it hard to accept anyone who isn't. You realize the one you met earlier wasn't after you, he was assigned to destroy the spirit trapping your mind. You were just in his way and he wanted to show you that you were fighting yourself. He got angry when you showed me and Zion disrespect."

"I'm sorry. I had lost my mind and didn't care who I hurt." Griffin admitted.

"You're forgiven. It's time we strengthened your spirit, but your body needs to eat before you get another headache," Jesus urged.

"I didn't bring any food with me," Griffin confessed.

Jesus didn't hesitate, "I always come prepared, look out your window."

When Griffin looked outside, the angel who was still parading around as his twin stood next to an open fire that had a rabbit roasting on a spit. The angel also had sweet potatoes roasting on coals. Some he'd gathered out of Griffin's grandmother's old garden. The sight of the meal made Griffin's stomach growl and his mouth water. He was hungry and wanted all the blessing prepared for him.

While Griffin and Jesus ate a meal together, Griffin has his spirit renewed. He had many questions were answered about his upbringing.and the traditions he'd followed. When Griffin asked about his mother's well-being, Jesus told him she would need to find her own way to God's kingdom.

When Jesus saw the worry on Griffin's face, he explained to him there wasn't anything he could do to change his mother's mind, but not to worry. We knew Irene wouldn't listen to him, and he would be wasting his breath. We had something else planned to bring her around. Irene was dead set against Odette, and she would blame her for taking Griffin away from his roots.

Throughout the night and into the next day, one childhood hurt after another was erased by an explanation from Jesus. Once Griffin gathered the strength to ask Jesus about his future, he was told it was up to him. Jesus' comment made Griffin think, and with a renewed excitement, he asked,"will you help me find Odette? I'm eager to share my life with the two of you."

Jesus replied, "take care of business first. Don't leave your livelihood undone. File a claim with the insurance adjusters then release your Uncle Randy from jail."

"Why should I give Randy mercy?" Griffin asked.

"Because I gave it to you. Let go of all your hurts and ill feelings, they only keep you bogged down in self-pity. Walk with me in love and forgiveness towards everyone, even if it hurts," Jesus urged.

Griffin followed Jesus' instructions and had Randy released from jail. He wasn't allowing anything to disconnect his flow with love and his new-found relationship with Jesus. He cherished his born-again experience. Randy was grateful and promised not to interfere in Griffin's life again. The stay in jail helped Randy to see his destructive ways. The days he'd spent in jail was to his advantage, the sobriety Randy gained helped Griffin lose some of his hate against the old man.

Each day after that, Griffin purposely conversed and asked Jesus to guide his steps, so he wouldn't fall into self-works again. He also had to rely on their constant communication to keep him from getting impatient and running off to find Odette.

Jesus worked alongside Griffin for almost two weeks before Griffin was ready to leave Oklahoma. Each day Griffin muddled through legalities, finances, insurance, or inventory issues that were the details he had to attend to that would help his future.

After arranging all his affairs, Griffin had one other task and that was to make peace with his mother and inform her of his plans. She wouldn't be happy with his news and Griffin knew she would make a fuss, but he was determined to find Odette. She would eventually have to give in because it was a fight she could not win. Irene was furious! She didn't want Griffin to leave Oklahoma.

The day Griffin was to leave town, we had to soften Irene's heart a little. We wanted her to give Griffin at least a word of encouragement to send him forward. It wasn't our plan for either of them to have animosity in their hearts. They had to part on good terms or another evil spirit would try and make a home in their soul. Neither knew what lie ahead, but we knew it would be many months before Griffin saw his mother again.

Confused

I kept a diligent watch over Odette while Jesus was with Griffin. For the first week after leaving Oklahoma, she agreed to stay with her parents until her stitches had to be removed, only to keep them from worrying about her health.

It wasn't long after they arrived home that their church counselor visited their house. Odette didn't want therapy to help her deal with emotions, but to appease her parents, she agreed to attend their church counselor's sessions twice a week to help her sort through decisions she had to make.

Loneliness like she'd never known engulfed Odette when she returned to her apartment. So, the next morning she made an appointment with the counselor and realized after the first few minutes of her session that she'd made another mistake. He only made her feel worse. The counselor was not sympathetic to her broken heart, he immediately began to condemn her behavior and threw out scriptures about a sinful lifestyle. Odette couldn't believe his harsh accusations and she refused to make another appointment for more of his abuse. Instead of feeling encouraged, she left his office feeling dirty.

Odette rode around town, she didn't want to go back to the apartment. She needed a sympathetic ear and wanted someone to bare her soul to, so I urged her to seek counsel from her.mother.

I had a reason for this, Mrs. Payne had to shed light on another love story, and it would be the perfect time to clear the air and help Odette change her mind about leaving Griffin. The love story she must share would prove to Odette that she wasn't crazy. It would also set the stage for Odette's new revelations.

Mrs. Payne was happy to see her daughter when she arrived at the house. "Hi, honey. What do I owe for this visit?

Odette confessed, "Mom, I need to talk with someone who won't judge me. Will you listen to me and help me make the right decisions?"

"I'll do the best I can, but I thought Counselor Roberts was helping you sort things out," her mother said.

Odette blurts, "he's a jerk. He practically called me a whore and wouldn't listen to me, all he wanted to do was shove scriptures down my throat and accuse me of loose living. The last thing I should be accused of is being promiscuous, Griffin was my first in every way."

Mrs. Payne asks, "do feel ashamed?"

"Not at all. I am a level-headed woman who went into the love affair with my eyes open," Odette answered.

"Do you love Griffin?" Her Mom asked.

Odette began to cry and shook her head, "yes, with all my heart, I don't want to annul the marriage. If there weren't a child involved, I'd fight tooth and nail to save our marriage."

"Child or no child, you need to fight," Mrs. Payne urged.

Odette was stunned at her mother's statement, "You think I should fight for him? I thought you were against the marriage."

Mrs. Payne stood and gazed out the kitchen window. Then she lowered her head with her back still turned away from

Odette and said softly, "I'm not against your marriage at all. In fact, I feel it's God's way of righting a prior wrong in our family's history."

"What family wrong, Mom?" Odette asked.

Mrs. Payne grabbed a cup of coffee and offered Odette a cup before sitting down at their kitchen table to answer the question. "Honey, look at me. What do you see at first glance?

Confused by her mom's question, Odette said, "I see a lovely black-haired woman."

"Exactly! You see black hair. Do you want to know why I have black hair when everyone on my mother's side of the family has red hair, and your grandfather's family have light brown hair?" Her Mom explained.

"I don't understand," Odette confesses.

Mrs. Payne takes a gulp of coffee then says, "Grandpa is not my daddy. He adopted me when I was two years old after he married Grandma. We've kept this secret from you, not because I'm ashamed of Grandma, but because we try not to bring her pain. Plus, I owed it to your Grandpa not to continually make an issue of my true heritage, he's the only daddy I've ever known."

"I'm listening, tell me everything," Odette said.

Her Mom continues, "Grandma was nineteen when she ran away from Albany with a man. She met Chad Clearwater at one of Albany's Indian Festivals. He and his family traveled in a Native American Festival circuit and Mama was smitten with him instantly.

Chad was tired of traveling and the two of them ran away together without their families' permission, and she became pregnant with me soon after. When the families located the two of them, Chad's family was adamant that he leave your Grandma and he rebelled. A fight between him and his dad ended badly, and Chad fell on a sharp object and suffered a fatal injury. He died in front of Grandma.

Grandma didn't tell her parents about the pregnancy until she was too big to deny it. When I was born, she refused to place me up for adoption. She raised me as a single mom without parental support until she met Grandpa. He made her see she was worth loving and in time, she fell in love with him, but it wasn't the same kind of love she had for Chad. Even today she will tell you that his death still hurts and haunts her."

"How did she keep that secret from Grandpa? Wasn't he jealous?" Odette asked.

"Your Grandpa knows, he accepted the fact that Grandma was traumatized. He is not jealous of a ghost. He truly loves Grandma and me, and when Grandma gets melancholy, he arranges for her to have a two-week vacation at the beach where she and Chad lived. The beach is the only place Grandma regains her peace," her Mom reveals.

Odette was shocked but curious to know more, "I knew Grandma loved the beach and liked to go there by herself, but I didn't know why. Did her vacations really help?"

"Immensely. After each trip, she returned home energized and grateful to have the life she was given," her Mom shared.

Raven H. Price

"Do you think if I went to the beach for a few weeks I would get a new perspective? I can't relax at home," Odette asks her Mom.

Her Mom replies, "It can't hurt. You have another month before school starts, so take the chance. There is no greater counsel than listening to your own heart. At the beach, you won't have outsiders making decisions for you. Go! You'd make Grandma proud."

"What beach did Grandma visit? I want to commune in the same place with nature and talk to God," Odette inquired.

Her Mom answers, "Panama City Beach, Florida. It's a huge vacation spot for tourist. I'll call Grandpa and ask who he rents the condominium from. I won't tell him about you and Griffin, I'll leave that up to you. I know he will gladly help you. We can count on him to make this happen. Go home and pack and I'll call you with the details."

Odette rushed home and began packing. She was zipping up the last suitcase when her mother called with details and a surprise for Odette. When Mrs. Payne explained to Grandpa that Odette needed to find God, he gave in and told another secret. He owned the condominium. He'd purchased it for Grandma as a loving gesture to use when she needed during the spring and summer months. Then he rented it during the fall and winter months as an investment. He was happy to let Odette stay there for as long as she needed and wanted her to consider the stay as an early birthday gift from her Grandparents.

By 4:00 p.m. that day, Odette was at The Long Beach Resort at Panama City Beach and entered Grandma's condominium. Her place was a corner, one-bedroom condominium with a balcony facing the beach. Odette instantly fell in love with the tiny condominium. Everything inside of it reminded her of her sweet grandparent. Stepping out on the balcony, Odette saw the beach for the first time. It was breathtaking and would be the perfect place for her to seek her heart's desire.

Remembering Zion

Before Odette unpacked her things, she rushed down to the beach and walked along the shore amazed at the clear, emerald green waters and the snow-white sand. She'd never been to the gulf coast of Florida before. It was a magical place, but she understood why the family went to other beaches.

Odette's mother would insist they go to Daytona Beach, or beaches on Georgia's Atlantic coast whenever they wanted a beach vacation because she didn't want to remember what happened to her mother. Those places were nice, but the waters there weren't as clear or the sand as white and she understood why the Gulf of Mexico was Grandma's special place.

Back in the condominium, Odette searched through some brochures Grandma had lying around that advertised good places to eat and ordered takeout from an Oyster Bar close by. To pass the time while her meal was being prepared, she went to the Wal-Mart across the street from the condominiums and purchased the supplies and groceries she needed for her stay. For the first time since leaving Oklahoma, her mind wasn't consumed with worry.

After placing the groceries in her pantry, Odette took the hot seafood platter to the balcony to watch the waves and quietly ate her dinner. She also loved watching the waves and tourist below. The evening was warm and she relaxed while sipping a glass of wine. The calmness allowed her to release some of the pain and hurtful feelings she'd held against Jesus and her new friend, Zion. The solace made her realize that she missed them.

Instead of calling out to Jesus or Zion after the revelation, Odette sat on the balcony to watch some children play as the sun slowly went down in the west. The children's joyful laughs and play brought joy to her as they chased fiddler crabs along the beach.

Watching them made Odette wonder what her children would be like and she pictured a small black-haired daughter in her mind who ran with the crowd of kids. The thought jolted her back into reality and it forced her to admit to herself that she wanted a family with Griffin. With that thought lodged in her mind, she went inside and prayed for Zion or Jesus to help.

Zion pulled away from Abba and shouted, "Odette is calling out to me! She is thinking about me in a nice way and wants a friend to help."

"We knew she would come around," Abba states.

"Let me go to her. Please, pretty please. I can be the friend she needs," Zion begged.

Abba looked at Zion and said, "don't get carried away. Go slowly with her and listen more than talk. Can you do that?"

"I'll do the best I can to help her through the confusions she has," Zion agrees.

Abba urges, "Go to her, then!"

Odette was having her morning coffee on the balcony when Zion rode in on a cool breeze and sat in a chair next to her. She didn't manifest in human form right away, she remained still and listened to Odette's thoughts for a long time until she was sure Odette wanted to talk.

I knew exactly when Zion's cue to speak showed up. Odette spotted two dolphins swimming in front of the condominiums and thought to herself, *'I wonder if dolphins mate for life?'*

Zion didn't want to frighten Odette, so she moved in her chair just enough for it to make a sound on the concrete deck. When Odette's gaze turned to see what moved, Zion made her appearance. "Hello, dear. May I join you? I couldn't help but overhear your thoughts about dolphins and if they stay with the same mate for life."

Odette's expression change immediately. Her heart was soaring, happy that Zion came because of her prayers. It was good to see her mentally respond in a good way. "Yes, please join me! We need to talk."

"How can I help you, Odette?" Zion asked.

Odette's face changed from happy to sad, instantly, and tears began to flow down her cheeks, "can you explain what happened to me? I thought Jesus assured me that Griffin and I were to be together forever."

Zion answered, "He did. I was there when he said it."

"Then what happened? Why did Griffin abandon me?" Odette asked.

"He didn't abandon you. Legalities got in his way," Zion answered truthfully.

"What do you mean?" Odette asked.

"You left the hospital before he could prove to the hospital authorities that the two of you were married. The hospital refused him any access to your room because the police were involved and he didn't have another way to contact you. Neither one of you had the necessary information about the other and one thing lead to another," Zion informs.

Odette mused, "I was so hurt. When I couldn't reach him, I assumed he'd abandoned me when he didn't visit. What did we do wrong?"

Zion began to rattle off details, "Lust happened, Odette. The two of you were more caught up in physical pleasures than getting to know each other. Basic details were left undone because your hormones ran the show. You can explain every detail about each other's body, but you know nothing about each other's soul. You failed to fall in love with the other's personality and the trials of life began to test you,"

"Will we ever see each other again so we can remedy that?" Odette inquired.

"Eventually, be patient. What God has put together, nothing can separate," Zion shared.

Odette inquired further, "Should I return to Oklahoma and try and find Griffin?"

"No, remember what Jesus told you, it's the man's job to find a wife, not a woman's responsibility to seek a mate. I can assure you, Griffin will find you. Give him time to track you down.

In a panic, Odette asks, "how will he find me? He doesn't know anything about me, he doesn't have my address, phone number, or my parent's name and address"

"As I sit here with you explaining the details, Jesus is helping Griffin face what happened. Trust in our process. You'll want a partner committed to our ways and by the time Griffin finds you again, you can be assured he won't leave you before knowing more than just what you look like," Zion assured.

Relieved by Zion's answer, Odette changed topics, "you said you heard my thoughts about dolphins earlier. Do they mate for life?"

Zion giggled, "No. They may have many sexual partners throughout their lives, but they will make friends with others for life."

Odette pondered Zion's comment, then she inquired, "you have a point to share, don't you?"

Zion's laughter rang throughout the atmosphere. She was in her natural element and enjoying the banter with Odette, and it was making Abba smile while He watched from above.

"Hormones rule animals and most people, but when humans accept their spiritual existence they are no longer like animals. Their spiritual identity with God will rule their thoughts and actions because they'll remember the truth; that they are created in His image and likeness.

Soulmates are more like best friends than sexual partners, and they survive by a spiritual connection to another's heart and mind. Plus, they understand that the body's urge to have sex won't last forever. What they count on is trust."

"You have a point. I see where Griffin and I failed. Other than the visit we had with you and Jesus in our hotel suite, we spent most of the time learning how to please our bodies. We role-played a lot and had no serious conversations.

The night we married, I didn't understand why he was distant towards me. I wanted him to talk about his feeling, but he wouldn't share his thoughts. I felt shut out, unnecessary and it hurt my feelings," Odette confessed.

Zion frankly asked, "I have a question for you. If you couldn't see Griffin's face or body anymore, would you feel the same way about him? What if he became maimed and couldn't perform sexually again, would it matter to you?"

Odette's face paled. She thought for a few moments then answered truthfully, "I'm not sure. It was his beauty that first grabbed my attention and his loving making that had me dazzled."

Zion's wisdom enlightens Odette further, "If you want a happy marriage, then you have a job to do when the two of you meet again. It's important to find the spirit man inside the body and fall in love with him. You already know how to please his body, it's up to you to sew his heart to yours.

The two of you didn't heed our warnings. When we spoke with you in the woods and told you what to do, you only shared what you accomplished in life and nothing further. When trials showed up after you married, you couldn't mentally connect, and you didn't know why. Knowing what someone has does not tell you how or why they have it.

A couple's emotions during trials make a difference in a trial's outcome. Caring for the other will help to calm emotions rather than tackling the trial. A couple's mental bond has the power to change their situations. The pressures of life are real and hard to endure without a companion's loving support; iron sharpens iron. Encouragement and faith in each other will speak in power.

Listen to my words, flesh fails, but a being's spirit never will, and that's what dolphins understand and what makes them some of the smartest animals God and I created. They depend on friends more than sexual encounters and they live in peace.

When hormonal lust rules a person mind and emotions, they don't have peace, and lust creates jealousy instead of stability. It takes trust to endure life's challenges, not sex or education,"

"Affairs are encouraged?" Odette asked.

Zion laughed, "Heaven forbid. What I'm saying is that if someone is unfaithful it was due to a flesh failure, not a spiritual failure. Hormones make people do stupid things. Life's trials have a way of separating a couple when the going gets tough and sex can't solve any of those issues. Mental support and understanding each other's faults is necessary to overcome daily tests.

It's important to make time for intimacy. Intimacy is not only sexual, though, it is getting naked with your feelings and emotions, so you can communicate with each other and speak in line with God's ways. A man will need sex more than a woman, but they may also need a listening ear from someone who cares about their feelings. Neither will know what makes the other tick if they don't talk.

Griffin has not sought attention outside of marriage, if he had, forgiveness would be necessary. It is important to remember that trust can be rebuilt if you understand flesh cannot be controlled without a relationship with Jesus. Allow Jesus to teach you self-control. If He can forgive those who murdered Him, then He can help someone forgive unfaithfulness."

"Aren't you teaching me?" Odette asked.

Zion answers, "Jesus had to save me. I'm not qualified to save. I'm only telling you to trust Him for yourself. He's the anchor, remember."

After their first morning together, Zion and Odette were inseparable. It was God's plan for them to bond while they waited for Griffin and Odette to reunite.

After reuniting, each day, the two women talked, shopped, walked the beach when Odette's knee didn't hurt, and they enjoyed meeting other people. It gave Zion her heart's desire and Odette a chance to have a motherly friend who could give truthful advice. All of it was making Abba happy. He could hear wisdom sing in the ocean breeze.

Searching For Odette

Griffin and Jesus enjoyed the two-and-a-half day trip to Georgia. They discussed many of the same things Zion and Odette talked about concerning sex and communication. Points about emotional energies and happiness were also discussed and how they exude a positive power when a couple's lives are based on a trust in Him.

Griffin admitted he had trust issues with people, and he preferred spending time with animals. When Griffin shared the information with Jesus it opened a door for him to ask about wolves and swans having soulmates.

Jesus was impressed that Griffin wanted to know. He confirmed that the animals were monogamous creatures, but entirely different. Wolves ran in packs because they were highly social creatures and loved being together with other wolves. Swans didn't need a flock to live in peace, two were happy together, but they preferred banding together in groups only for protection and finding places to feed.

Griffin was puzzled by that information, and asked, "I thought Odette was more like a swan, but she isn't, I am. She will need friends, won't she?"

"Yes. Odette is a very social young lady. Even though she did not date, her days were filled communicating with people. That is why she teaches, she loves the interaction. Since you prefer being alone, you tend to use people and leave them when your need for them is met," Jesus answered truthfully.

Griffin admits, "I may have a problem sharing Odette's attention with others."

"It's something you'll have to work on, Griffin. Odette is the type of lady who won't cheat on you sexually, but she will seek verbal stimulation with others if you aren't open with her. She will only feel secure if she knows she has the key to your heart and mind. She must trust you. If you can't share your feelings she won't feel like she is your soulmate," Jesus advised.

Changing the subject, Griffin inquired, "what should I do when we get to Albany. Should I locate every Payne I find listed in a phone book?"

Jesus chuckled. then asked, "do you remember anything Odette said about her family? Is there anything you can use to save time searching?"

"She talked about their Sunday lunches. They would go out to eat after church," Griffin shared.

Jesus asked him, "do you remember what church they attended?"

Griffin palmed his forehead and squeezed, "I can't remember the name of it, but I recall her saying it was a Baptist church. She didn't like it because it was a small church full of old people and nothing like the one she visited at college."

"Then I suggest you find a hotel in Albany with Wi-Fi and do some research for Baptist churches. You may recall the name of it," Jesus said.

At lunch, Griffin used his phone and searched for hotels in the Albany area that had Wi-Fi and other comforts he liked and made the reservation before resuming the drive. On Wednesday, at 2:00 p.m, Oklahoma time, Griffin pulled into Albany's Hilton Gardens tired and road weary. He didn't bother to unpack right away, but he made sure his phone was charging while he took a nap. He would begin the research when he woke.

Two hours later, Griffin rose from his nap and began the research for churches. The number of churches in the town flabbergasted him. One by one, he researched information to see if he could find a clue. About an hour into the search, he remembered Odette saying it was a small church located in the country outside of town.

Numb from researching, Griffin took a break and ordered a sandwich from room service. He didn't want to leave his room to find food. When the waiter arrived with his meal, Jesus whispered in his ear, "ask him if he knows of a small Baptist church in the country."

The waiter was very helpful, and Griffin tipped him well. He gave Griffin three choices to visit, so he discontinued his search. He was tired but couldn't rest. With nothing to occupy his mind, Griffin left the room and took a walk along Front Street until he found a bench. The bench faced the Flint River and while he watched the water flow he d pondered over his life.

The roaring waters reminded him of the stories his mother told him about the Creek Indians who used to live near the Flint River in Georgia. It was ironic that he was sitting in the areas he'd always heard about. He was in the Creeks natural habitat, so he let his mind wander, remembering what Jesus said about Odette being a social creature. He asked himself if could move to Albany and stake a claim on some of the land instead of uprooting her away from her friends and family.

When Griffin returned to the hotel, he quickly went to sleep once he laid on the bed and he slept until morning. During the night, he dreamed that he and Odette were natives living in a hut next to the Flint River. She taught a pack of wolves and he canoed in the river with two swans. The dreams were peaceful with no dramatic influences that made him toss or turn, so when he was jolted from sleep by a slamming door next to his room, he knew right away he had the answer to the previous night's question. He would be moving to Georgia and reclaiming some historical property for his ancestors and for his own children.

I watched as a thought registered in his mind, *'children!' I could be a dad.'* The remembrance of the failed prophylactic is of what prompted him to marry and it set fuel to his desire to find Odette.

Quickly dressing, Griffin went to the hotel restaurant to eat breakfast, so he could begin the search for Odette. While waiting for his meal, the angel assigned to watch over Griffin prompted him to Google on his cellphone 'Odette Payne, Albany, GA' to see what would come on the site. Griffin was shocked! Odette's picture came across the Android phone he was holding, she had a Facebook account, all he had to do was log in and he could see her posts.

Griffin couldn't remember how to log into the site. He never used social media. Lucy created media sites for his business and had fun making one for Facebook. He racked his brain for a memory of what she used for his Identification and password. He hadn't been interested in her playing around that day. Now, he wanted to kick his butt for not paying attention. The site asked for an email an possible ID. He entered his email, then he remembered when he and Lucy talked about his first patient at the clinic and typed the name Smokey, as the password. Instantly he was on the site. *It was a miracle*, he thought.

Odette's Facebook page showed him pictures of events, photos taken of her friends, the school, and kids she taught, and a few pictures of her parents. Looking through a long list of people on her site, he found the name of her dad. The long list of friends just proved she was definitely a social butterfly in the area. But, the site didn't show was what he needed most, an address or email account for her, so he did the only thing he could, he sent her a friend request, and prayed that she would check the site and know he was looking for her. Until then, he would use the information about her dad and try to track her down.

Griffin stopped at the front desk after eating and asked the hotel clerk if they had directory assistance, so he could locate Odette or Herman Payne. The clerk's eyes brightened when Griffin asked about Odette and Herman Payne and he answered, "I know Mr.and Mrs. Payne. Mr. Payne is on the town council and he attends meetings here in our hotel lounge each month. I met Mrs. Payne through him, they are lovely people, but I don't know Odette."

"Do you know how I can get in touch with Mr. Payne?" Griffin asked, again.

The clerk hesitated. He liked the Paynes and wanted to protect their privacy, so he asked, "Sir, will you please tell me why you need to talk with them? They are nice people and I don't want trouble."

Since the incident at the hospital, Griffin was ready. He was prepared with the necessary paperwork to prove who Odette was to him. He pulled an envelope from his pants pocket and showed the clerk who he was. Then he told the man a white lie saying she was missing and he had to tell her parents that he couldn't find her.

The clerk believed most of Griffin's story. Just to be safe, he pulled a large phonebook out from under the counter and turned through the pages. When he found Herman Payne's name, he didn't give Griffin the information, he called their home phone number himself and asked for Mr. Payne. When he had him on the phone, the clerk identified himself as the hotel clerk and told Mr. Payne that Griffin Waters needed to speak with him about his daughter.

Mr. Payne agreed to speak with Griffin, and the clerk handed the phone to Griffin and walked away, so he could privately talk with Mr. Payne. Before losing his nerve, Griffin introduced himself to the person on the phone and explained to him that he had to find Odette. He was surprised that Mr. Payne wasn't angry with him. When he explained why he couldn't visit Odette in the Hospital Mr. Payne was very nice and said he understood. Griffin's heart began to race with happiness from the warm welcome. He hoped Mr. Payne would let him see Odette, but his hopes were dashed when Mr. Payne said Odette was on another vacation to clear her head and decide what to do about their marriage, Griffin's heart sank to his shoes. The only thing that kept him from going insane was an invitation to have dinner with the Paynes and a promise to help him locate Odette.

Charlene Payne entered the kitchen just as her husband finished speaking with Griffin. "Who did you invited to dinner, Herman?" She asked.

"Our son-in-law, Griffin Waters. He is trying to find Odette. He explained to me why he didn't visit her in the hospital. Apparently, they'd only been married a few hours when Odette had the accident and he didn't have proof of marriage to show his connection to her. When they admitted her to the Intensive Care Unit, due to a violent experience, the hospital policy was to protect the patient, so Griffin had no choice but to wait until the Magistrate Judge could give him their Certificate of Marriage.

I'd like to meet the man who captured Odette's heart. He convinced me that he loves her. Instead of giving him her whereabouts, I thought you'd like to talk with him too," Herman admitted.

"Oh, my Lord," Charlene expressed.

A Glimmer of Hope

Griffin didn't like staying cooped in his hotel room, so he decided to go shopping for new clothes to impress his in-laws. He found his way to Albany's local mall and walked around a bit before going into one of the department store chains.

Jeans were his first pick, then he noticed a mannequin dressed in khakis and a knit shirt and thought those clothes would make a better first impression. Frustrated, he cried out in his mind, '*I could use a woman's touch, someone, who could help me impress Odette's parents*'.

Zion could hardly believe her ears when she overheard Griffin say he wanted help from a lady. '*Who better than she?*' She thought. So, while Odette was sunbathing, she quickly visited Abba and asked if she could barge in on Griffin's shopping spree and help him select an outfit.

Abba didn't mind. In fact, He was delighted Griffin desired help. It proved that his attitude had softened some and he'd be willing to allow Mother Earth back in his life the way she should be and not the way he was taught.

Zion approached Griffin slowly, so she wouldn't startle him, then she asked, "may I be of assistance Griffin? I do know a thing or two about fashion. I was the one who helped Odette find the dress she wore on your wedding day."

Griffin jumped when Zion spoke, but he quickly regained his composure and said, "I could use your help. Did Jesus send you?"

"No, Son. I overheard you say to yourself that you would like a lady's opinion about what to buy," Zion answered.

Griffin inquired, "Our thoughts are that naked to you guys? You hear everything we think as well as say. That's creepy."

"I'm sorry you feel that way, but we love you enough to desire the connection no matter how painful your thoughts may be to us," she countered.

Griffin knew he had touched a nerve that didn't need to be poked, so he changed the subject. "Then you know I have a dinner engagement with Odette's parents. I don't want to show up at their house wearing worn-out clothes. What should I buy, jeans or khakis, a knit shirt, or a cotton shirt? What kind of shoes?. I'm stumped."

"May I suggest you buy the khaki pants and pair it with a cotton shirt in a deep hue to match your skin tone. Odette's parents will be impressed. They have you pictured very differently," Zion shared.

"They know I'm Indigenous, don't they? So, they'll be expecting me to show up wearing jeans and boots. I like your plan. I'm far from the typical Indian who only hunts and fishes," Griffin agreed.

Zion smiled then said, "pair the outfit with soft leather loafers and you'll be fine. Don't forget to buy flowers for Mrs. Payne and you'll capture Mr. Payne's approval. I have to go now, but if you need me again, just think of me and I'll come running,"

Griffin bid her farewell and continued to shop. He chose a rust colored shirt that reminded him of Odette's wedding dress, a brown belt, and brown shoes to go with the khaki pants. After purchasing the outfit, he ate lunch and spent a few hours in the mail people watching. Studying the crowd, he understood that Georgia folks were no different than Oklahomans; people in the USA were the same.

Griffin couldn't believe how slow the day was moving and decided to go back to the hotel. Waiting in his room would make anxiety grow in his body and he knew he'd be a mess by nighttime if he didn't do something to release the tension. Pacing in the room, he stopped to look out the window and noticed a swimming pool and quickly used his pocket knife to make shorts out of the old jeans he wore since he hadn't packed a swimsuit.

He had the pool all to himself which made him happy. It allowed him time to think and not have to socialize. The water was cool and refreshing to his body, so he lapped around the pool until he tired of swimming. When he lies in a lounge chair it took only minutes for the warm sun to soothe away the tension and help him nap.

A kid jumped into the water and woke Griffin up. When he noticed he was no longer lying in the sunshine, it forced him to look at the time. He'd slept two hours and now had to rush to iron his new clothes, get ready, and find somewhere to buy flowers before dinner. The last thing he wanted was to be late.

Charlene Payne fretted over her dinner. When Herman came into the kitchen to check on her, he noticed she was acting strangely.

"Honey, why are you flustered?" He asked her.

She answered, "I don't know. I guess I'm worried what this man will want to know about us. I know I'm curious about him. Has it occurred to you that he is the only man Odette has ever been interested in? Why? What does he have that no other man possessed?"

As soon as the questions were spoken, the doorbell rang, and Herman went to meet Griffin. Charlene stayed in the kitchen and heard them speaking. She was pulling the roasted pork loin from of the oven when Herman led Griffin into the kitchen where she was.

"Honey, this is Griffin Waters, our son-in-law," Herman introduced.

Charlene stood up with roast in hand and turned to look at Griffin. She almost dropped the pan of meat on the floor when she saw him for the first time. I heard her thoughts loud and clear. '*No wonder he has Odette spellbound, he is gorgeous! A piece of art! Eye candy; chiseled face, tanned skin, tall and big-muscled.*

With her mouth dry, she managed to say, "Come in, Griffin. I've been dying to know who captured my daughter's heart."

Griffin handed her a bouquet of yellow roses, and said, "these are for you. A peace offering to say I'm sorry for the mess I've made of things."

Herman was impressed by Griffin's gesture of flowers for Charlene, but he was more impressed to hear that his new family member wasn't a bum. Over their meal, Herman learned that Griffin was a respectable Veterinarian in Oklahoma and well established. It proved to him that Odette used smarts in choosing a mate and hadn't just fallen for the man's physique.

Later that evening, while the three of them relaxed on the patio, eating peach pie, and drinking coffee Griffin remembered he had the two charms Zion had left in his apartment. Standing, he dug through his pants pocket for the charms. When he found them, he handed them to Mrs. Payne, "these are Odette's. I found them in my apartment a few days after her accident. I knew they were hers because I saw them on a bracelet she wore on our wedding day. I'm curious, are they family heirlooms?"

Charlene looked at the small golden charms in her hand, and almost burst into tears, but held her composure. Memories rushed back, and she answered softly, "these charms belonged to my Mother. She gave them to Odette when she left for college as a reminder of who truly anchors our heart and who she must form her life after. These charms are Christian symbols that our family use to keep us grounded in the love God has for us, and how we need to love others like he does. I'm happy you found them. I'm sure she doesn't know they are lost."

Griffin softly mudders, "I recently received Jesus as my savior. Odette convinced me he was real. Come to think about it, I think she said something about how He stabilized her heart and gave her an example for living. I didn't know He represented an anchor for our souls, though, that's good to know."

Charlene handed the charms back to Griffin and told him to keep them safe for Odette instead of keeping them herself. His statement of faith, finally made her feel comfortable enough to ask him a sensitive question. "Griffin, do you have another woman pregnant with your child? Odette is confused, that is why she is on vacation. We encouraged her to do some soul searching before annulling your marriage."

Griffin almost choked on his sip of coffee. He exclaimed,"Mrs.Payne I assure you Lois is not pregnant! When I confronted her about what happened she admitted to me that she only wanted to rile Odette, so she would fight her. I was never in love with that woman."

Charlene relaxed and asked another question, "if I tell you where to find Odette, then what? Will you track her down and provoke a fight or do you want to prove your intentions in a loving manner?"

Griffin didn't waste time, he answered quickly, "I can hardly breathe without her. I'll do anything to win her back. Please, tell me where to find her and what I should do."

"Griffin, I am a romantic by nature. I'm convinced you love Odette, but I don't know if she is ready to talk. I don't want her spooked by a phone call. If I were in her place, it would impress me more if you showed up on my doorstep instead of calling. If you called me, it would only create mental anguish until I saw you. I'd be thinking about what to say to you. A person's thoughts are their own worst enemy, she may run from you instead of communicating, don't allow her that chance. Find her!"

"I'll do anything. I need to see her," Griffin answered.

Happy with Griffin's answer, Charlene went inside the house and came back with the name and address of the Long Beach Resort written on a piece of paper. She leaned over and kissed Griffin on the cheek and said, "go get your woman, Griffin. You'll have to check into the resort, they won't allow you entrance unless you are a customer and I doubt they'll care one way or another if you say you're married to Odette. We won't interfere, we'll be praying for the success of your reunion, you're in God's care now. .Go with the flow, don't fight it.

Griffin left his in-laws house, feeling invigorated by their advice and excited he'd be seeing Odette soon. He wanted to drive straight to Florida, but it would be too late by the time he got there to check into a beach resort. He decided to stay one more night at the Hilton Gardens, and communicate with his anchor, then leave early the next day.

In Need of the Anchor

Odette met a lovely widow and her three small children while sunbathing next to the resort's pool. Sally Jenkins was a young woman who married a soldier and quickly became a mother. Each time her husband returned home from a tour of duty, she'd get pregnant. The last time she gave birth, she had twin girls, but before her husband had a chance to see them, he was killed overseas.

Odette bonded quickly with Sally. Conversations with her made Odette understand she had been grief-stricken like her new friend. Sally was a good diversion to keep her from worrying, she'd been at the beach for two weeks and still no word from Griffin. She wanted to have faith in what Zion said, but found it hard.

Sally only had a few days of vacation time and had to leave Saturday morning, so she and Odette decided to enjoy the time together at the beach until then. Being together helped. Talking kept their minds free from self-pity while the kids enjoyed swimming and playing in the sand

The days they spent together were fun, but at night Odette wrestled with demons in her sleep. They tried to convince her that Griffin should be dead to her. The nightmare woke her up. Zion came quickly and tried to give comfort, but failed to squash Odette's fear. Frustrated that Odette couldn't hear her words, Zion relents, "Odette, dear. If you can't hear me, you have no other alternative but talk with Jesus. He's the only man who can help. Cry out to Him."

"Why? You're here what's the difference?" Odette inquired.

Zion sighs, "I can't prove things to you. I'm not human, Jesus is. Like I said earlier I'm not qualified to explain a human condition."

"I don't understand, you look human to me," Odette replied.

To answer Odette's question, Zion changed her form several times; a dog, cat, snake, and otter. Then she changed into fish flopping out of the water. To make her point very clear, she punched Odette in the face with a blast of icy wind and then rained on her head with warm water.

"See my dear. I am anything I want to present. I am the universe and earth all combined. Jesus is the only God who was willing to give up his god-like condition to become human. He truly understands you, I can't. I'm frustrated because I can't help," Zion confessed.

Odette wiped the tears from her face and admitted why she hadn't desired Jesus' company. She felt he wouldn't understand her emotional behavior like a woman would. She said to Zion, "I've been a fool, haven't I? You told me you weren't qualified, now, I truly understand why you can't save my soul. I appreciate you trying, though."

Zion answered, "I'll leave the two of you alone. I need to visit Abba anyway, so I can calm down."

As soon as Zion exited, Odette took a deep breath and prayed, "Jesus, it's time we talked. I've allowed evil to play in my head long enough. I need your forgiveness and peace."

Faster than a blink, Jesus was standing in front of Odette with His arms opened wide. "Come here, Odette. What can I help you with?"

Odette ran into his arms, "Lord, I'm plagued by fear. I am having a hard time believing what you told me. Zion tried to help, she explained a lot to me, but I still lose faith. If God placed Griffin and I together then why aren't we?"

Jesus gently pushed Odette's away, so He could look into her eyes. Taking her hand, He motioned for them to sit on the bed. "You have to practice patience, my dear. We haven't lied to you. Griffin had his own demons to fight. We are all working on this together, it takes time to make things right."

"Waiting is hard," Odette admits.

"I know it is. I can tell you how to pass the time if you are willing to try." He advised.

"How?" She willingly asked.

"Focus on enjoying your life instead of worrying and entertaining your troubles. Make every second count by making others happy. This will change the energies around you and keep dark thoughts at bay. In no time, you'll find someone to encourage, it's fun and productive at the same time, and before you know it, your own happiness will arrive." Jesus explained.

Jesus' explanation snapped Odette out of her doldrums. Their conversation became light and upbeat after He told her what to do. She told Him about Sally and how they'd passed their time. He asked, "the day went quickly, didn't it? Now you know why. Spend this last day with her and the children, laugh and have fun. Joy attracts great things."

Odette looks at the floor and shyly says, "stay close by me. Zion was right, you make me feel so much better. I'm sorry for turning my back on you when all that happened to me. I shouldn't have blamed you for the mess."

Instead of saying a word in response, Jesus gave Odette a hug confirming that He appreciated her confession.

Griffin was up before daybreak, he showered and quickly packed. He didn't even take time to eat breakfast, and hastily checked out of his room. In his truck, he programmed the GPS with the address Mrs. Payne provided for Panama City Beach. He was well into the drive when the sun came up and he only stopped once when his stomach cried for food.

He pulled into a fast food place for a restroom break and food. He ordered two breakfast sandwiches and coffee to go and quickly resumed the journey. To pass the time, while he drove, he talked with Jesus, "I enjoyed meeting Odette's parents last night. They weren't anything like I imagined, though."

"What do you mean? Are you referring to their reactions towards you?" Jesus asks.

"No, they made me feel welcomed. It's not their reactions that have me confused," Griffin admits.

Jesus knew what had Griffin piqued, but He wanted him to say it aloud so they could talk about it. "Tell me, Griffin. Don't hold back."

"They didn't have red hair. Odette's is a flaming redhead. I'd pictured her mother to be an older version of her daughter. When she turned out to be dark haired it stumped me.

It made me focus on Mr. Payne's coloring, and he wasn't pale like Odette either. He was tanned. Why?" Griffin inquired.

Jesus laughed, "Flesh has a way of confusing people, but in all honesty, all of it is the same. Dirt is dirt, is it not? Odette's heritage is mixed dirt. She was made from the dust of Ireland, Scotland, England, Spain and Native America. What you see from skin tone will not explain ancestry, Mr. Payne is light skinned. He's only tan because he plays golf."

"Native American, who would have thought? I like the way you explain things to me. It makes sense. Odette is a puzzle for me to figure out. Does she know where she comes from?" Griffin asked.

"That's not for me to share. Find out for yourself. Like you stated, she's a puzzle. One God created for you to figure out," Jesus informed him.

Like Griffin hoped, conversing with Jesus on his journey to Florida made the time fly. He found the resort before they were open for business. Growling under his breath, he thought. *'What do I do now?'*

Griffin spotted a Wal-Mart across the street and decided to bide his time by walking around the store. He needed a few items anyway to make his stay at the beach easier. He found beach towels and picked out two, grabbed a bottle of tanning lotion, then picked out a swimsuit. He looked in the food section but decided not to purchase food until he knew more about his housing arrangements.

Confused about the time difference, he looked at his phone and saw that the time had changed back an hour from Georgia's time, it was 7:30 a.m instead of 8:30 and the resort office didn't open until 9:00 a.m.

To keep impatience at bay, Griffin ventured towards the sporting goods section and encountered a chatty stock clerk who asked if he was a tourist. Griffin explained that he'd never been to the ocean before, so the clerk recommended a pair of binoculars, gave Griffin a wink then suggested he spy on the female scenery that walked the beach.

Griffin knew what the clerk meant, but he wasn't interested in babe watching. He wanted to find Odette, but since the guy was nice and the binoculars were on sale, he put them in the buggy with his other items. Griffin didn't know it, but he engaged a guardian angel who was sent to encourage the purchase.

After shopping, Griffin drove back to the resort and waited for the opening time. He had another fifteen minutes before 9:00 a.m. As soon as a light turned on inside the office, he was at the door to get a room.

Jesus followed Griffin closely in the spirit realm, so He could see everything clearly. When He saw an evil spirit lingering in the shadows, He knew it was following Griffin and had plans to make him angry. Evil spirits were used to Griffin. His angry past preceded him, so Jesus instructed another angel to frighten the evil creature away.

A tiny lady greeted Griffin at the resort's information counter. When he inquired about a one-bedroom suite to rent, she politely told him there were no vacancies until Monday afternoon. In times past, Griffin's first reaction would have been to snap at the clerk and accuse her of lying, but because he'd given his heart to Jesus and had an angel's assistance to avert evil, he stayed calm enough to ask, "Can you help me find somewhere else to stay until then? I'll reserve one of your rooms and come back on Monday."

The lady smiled and said, "I'll try. We have two sister hotels down the road. Let me call one of them for you."

A few minutes later, the lady ask Griffin a question, "would you like a room beachside? The Majestic has a two-bedroom available."

"Tell them I'll take it!. Thanks," Griffin blurts.

On the way out of the office, Griffin remembered what Mrs. Payne said. She said don't fight, go with the flow. He'd never experienced easy transitions before this one and he liked it, especially when he saw that the Majestic was just as nice and only two buildings down the street from the Long Beach Resort.

Griffin carried all his gear inside the condominium and dropped everything into the master-bedroom; including the items, he'd just purchased. When he noticed the sliding glass door that exited onto a balcony, he quickly rushed outside and was stunned by the glorious view. Until that moment, he'd only seen pictures of the sea. The green-blue waters and white sand of the beach had him mesmerized more than the bikini-clad women walking along the beach. Suddenly, he was glad he purchased the binoculars. With them, he could see for miles up and down the emerald coastline.

"Jesus, I'm amazed by all your beauty. What a lovely place to reunite with Odette. I'm glad you came with me and made this trip easier," Griffin exclaims.

Jesus confesses, "You can thank my Father and Zion for the earth's beauty. Their love created a paradise for every living thing, didn't it? I'm happy you invited me to come with you, but it's my angels that help you move in our rhythm."

"Love created this beauty?" Griffin asked.

"Love, is all that matters, Griffin. It's why God sent me to save this world from eternal death. So many people were ruled by evil emotions before I came to influence their human conditions. People were created to share God's love with Him and each other. I had to repair the breach that kept mankind away from Him in order for that to happen. God wants men and women to know true love, so they can create beautiful children with Him." Jesus shares.

"I want nothing more than that with Odette. Will I have to wait much longer?" Griffin asked.

Jesus laughs, "Again, Griffin, that is entirely up to you. You know where she is. The beach isn't private. Use your new binoculars and look for your beloved, but keep your promise. Just don't rush her. Go slow like Mrs. Payne suggested. .I'll be nearby. Trust me to see you through. There will always be obstacles in the way, but when you believe I'm near and helping you overcome the obstacles, then you won't be bothered."

"Right… you are my anchor, here to keep my heart and mind steady. Good to know," Griffin states.

Spectacular Views

Griffin went inside the condominium and changed into his new swimsuit. It was too early to sunbath on the beach, so he grabbed a beach towel, binoculars, and found a spot at the Majestic's poolside to look for Odette.

Looking in Odette's direction with the binoculars, he was fascinated by the busy-work around her resort; people worked like ants. Proprietors had employees cleaning the pools, patios, and setting up lounge chairs with umbrellas. Places to relax were prepared on the decks and down on the beach in front of the condominium for the crowd that would swarm their area soon. He hoped one of those in the crowd would eventually be Odette.

It was around 10:00 a.m. when Griffin spotted a redheaded woman in a turquoise one-piece bathing suit playing with three small children on the beach. He adjusted his binoculars but couldn't tell if the lady was Odette. The woman looked happy playing with the children, so he considered her to be their mother. The sight of them playing was sweet and made him watch intently. He became enthralled by the view and his thoughts became very loud. He wanted a family and hoped to one day see Odette and their children play together like this little family.

When one of the little girls fell, skinned her knee, and started crying, the lady quickly scooped her up and ran back to the condominiums with the two other kids trailing her. Griffin's heart almost stopped. That's when he got a clear look at the woman's face; it was Odette.

He quickly stood and threw the binocular's strap over his shoulder and ran down on the beach in Odette's direction. When he rushed up to the resort's deck area, he was abruptly stopped.

The Security Guard ordered, "Mister, you can't come in here without an armband."

Quickly, Jesus whispers in Griffin's ear, "I'm working on this. Don't get angry. Apologise and walk away. The guard won't believe you if you try and explain."

Griffin obeyed but refused to leave the Long Beach Resort area. He walked up to a young man sitting in a booth on the beach, and asked if he could use one of their chairs and umbrellas, but was told they were for rent only. He thanked the guy and looked around for shade. There were a few palm trees near the hotel tall enough, so he moved under them and waited for Odette to appear again.

Griffin wasn't interested in talking with anyone, but he did enjoy Jesus' company. When he got too hot, he swam in the ocean. When sea creatures came into view, he viewed them with his binoculars and talked with Jesus about them. If he hadn't gotten thirsty, he could have stayed all day, enjoying the sites, but his body was too hot and weak to continue the stakeout.

When he returned to his room, he gulped water from the tap in his condominium until he was refreshed. He wanted to return quickly to his place on the beach and grabbed his wallet and another towel, so he could stay longer if necessary. A snack bar was located on his way, so he purchased two bottles of water, a packaged sandwich, and cookies to carry with him. But, by the time he had his supplies in hand, it was pouring rain and it was pointless to continue. He sighed because this was another obstacle, Florida's unpredictable weather.

The rain didn't stop until it was dark outside, but Griffin's heart stayed calm. To pass time, he drove back to the Wal-Mart, so he could buy food and drinks to last a few meals. He refused to be unprepared again and also purchased a small cooler to carry supplies down to the beach the next day. He could hardly wait to rent a lounge chair with umbrella on the beach, so he could wait comfortably for Odette to make another appearance.

Griffin ate a microwaved meal and settled out on the balcony with his wooden flute to ease his tension. Playing always calmed his nerves and settled his thoughts. To his surprise, people below his room shouted for him to play other tunes. It made his night pleasant.

Odette leaned against the railings of her condominium's balcony and starred up at the stars. With Jesus back in her life, she was happier than she'd been in weeks. The day had been fun with Sally and her kids. She'd made a friend for life. When the rain kept them off the beach, they took the kids to an indoor zoo down the street. The kids got to pet various birds and watch the zookeepers feed other animals. They didn't stop finding things to do together until the kids were too sleepy after dinner to continue.

Sally and Odette exchanged numbers and said their goodbyes when they returned to the resort. It would be too fast and furious in the morning to make another fun time happen before Sally and the kids had to check out. Walking away from her friends was the only sad thing in Odette's heart that evening.

Odette noticed that the beach below was clear of people and quiet for a change. The waves beaching the beach were only the things making noise. This wasn't the norm and Odette knew it. Remembering how Zion had punched her with a blast of wind, she questioned, "What's happening, Lord? It too quiet around here."

"Listen with your heart. Zion wants you to hear something beautiful," Jesus sweetly answered.

Odette sat in a chair on the balcony and closed her eyes. She didn't want anything to distract her from hearing what Zion wanted her to hear. Then she heard it! The unmistakable sound of a wooden flute. It made her heart race and hope return. Had Griffin come at last to find her? She asked Jesus and Zion the question, but they didn't reply, Odette was left to her own imaginations and could hardly rest all night from the excitement.

The next morning a little before daybreak, Odette grabbed a quick cup of coffee and ate a muffin. Then she jumped into her swimsuit, threw on a topper and rushed down to the pool to look at the people walking the beach. She prayed that her mind was not playing tricks on her. She was sure she had heard Griffin playing his flute somewhere close by. She knew this because it was the same song she'd heard him play the day after their first kiss.

The air was foggy, and Odette couldn't see very far in any direction, but that did not deter her from taking a steady visual at the resort's gate looking towards the beach. Straining her eyes and ears she listened and prayed for a miracle. Her eyes focused on someone walking towards her resort in the mist. The size of the man, his coloring, and his stride was unmistakable, it was Griffin!

With her heart beating in her throat, Odette could barely stand let alone run. It took a soft nudge from Jesus to give her strength, "Odette, don't be afraid of your husband. Just remember what Zion instructed. Make him work for your affections. Force him to know the real you and not just your body."

With Jesus' approval ringing in her ears, Odette took off running towards Griffin. Griffin had been lazily walking to the lounge chairs when someone running towards him made him stop in his tracks. When Griffin realized who it was, he couldn't believe the miracle. He dropped his cooler and began to run towards Odette like a madman.

Their bodies collided hard. Without wasting time apologizing, they found each other's mouth and kissed passionately. When they came up for air, each pulled away without letting go of their grip. Neither could speak because they didn't know what to say, so they glared into the other's eyes.

Griffin bent to kiss Odette again, but before he could, Zion, in the form of a dolphin, jumped in the water a few feet from where they stood. Instantly, Odette's mind returned, and she was able to push lust behind her. She pressed her hands on Griffin's chest and gently shoved. "Griffin, I love you, but I will not return to the way things were."

"I understand. We have a lot to discuss. How can I make it up to you, Odette? I can't stand another day without you," he stated.

Odette smiled and shyly demanded, "I want to be courted. Wine and dine me. I'd like to go dancing and do all the things I've missed doing as a teenager. Griffin, I never dated. I was too focused on school to seek a guy's attention. I don't know what it is like to have a boyfriend. I want to find out what you like to do, and I want you to know more about me than what I'm like in bed."

"Your wish is my command," he said with a smile.

Odette searched his eyes and knew he was sincere and not making fun of her request. Then she ordered, "kiss me, fool! Then we can start over by enjoying this beach."

Starting Over

Odette knew better than take Griffin up to her condominium, she didn't want to tempt lust. Instead, she led Griffin to the poolside deck, showed the Security Guard her armband and explained to him that Griffin was her guest for the day. Once Griffin had an armband of his own, they found two lounge chairs in a secluded area where they could watch the scenery and talk privately.

They discussed every detail of what happened before and after the accident. Griffin even explained how he tracked her down and that her parents had been very welcoming. They also talked about the emotional turmoils they faced without each other. Odette even found the courage to ask Griffin about Lois.

Odette closed the door on her suspicious mind when Griffin said there wasn't a relationship with Lois and no baby on the way. But, it only proved to her just how little she really knew about her husband. Trust took time to develop. Knowing a person's character was important and that was something she hadn't learned before marrying him.

When the area around the pool became overcrowded, they took a stroll hand-in-hand along the beach, so Griffin could show Odette where he was staying. He explained that he had a condominium reserved at the Long Beach but couldn't get in it until Monday. To calm Odette's mind, he quickly promised to maintain his own space until they decided what to do about their marriage arrangements.

He asked Odette if she would like to see his condominium and have a sandwich. She looked at him intently and said, "it's too soon for us to be near a bedroom. If you don't mind, I will rest by the pool until you bring me one."

"You may be right." Griffin agreed. "It's been hard for me to hide my need for you in this swimsuit. I probably couldn't control myself if I had you alone in my rooms."

Griffin ran upstairs, made sandwiches, and grabbed two bottles of water from the refrigerator before returning. Odette was talking with a ground's keeper when he found her again. Instantly, he felt a pang of jealousy grab his chest, but, before it festered, he cast the ugly thought aside and quickly thanked Jesus for placing a guardian angel around him. He knew the angel helped him stay calm so he could react peacefully, and in a loving manner, when trials formed by evil spirits raised their ugly heads.

He walked up to them and threw out his hand toward the man and said, "hi, my name is Griffin."

The man shook Griffin's hand and replied, "I'm Nathan Powell. I was explaining to this young lady that I think Uncle Ernie's is the best seafood restaurant in town. If you like adventure, take the boat to Shell Island, it's lovely. Or you can go on deep sea fishing trips if you life stuff like that. Panama City is loaded with things to do and places to see. That's why so many people visit."

To imitate a dance move, Griffin moved in a jerky manner and asked, "Where's a good place to go dancing? I want to show Odette all my moves."

The guy snickered at Griffin's attempt to prove he was a good dancer and said, "Club LaVela draws the younger crowd. Schooners and a couple of other places have bands geared to older tourist. I hope you too have fun."

After the man walked away, they sat and ate their meal. Due to not being able to sleep the night before, Odette was extremely tired after eating her sandwich. Her sluggish actions made Griffin ask if she were all right. She explained why she was tired and asked if she could return to her condominium for a nap. She wanted to be refreshed when they had their first date.

Griffin didn't want her out of his sight but knew he had to let her go. Deciding on 6:30 pm to start their date, he walked her back to the Long Beach Resort and watched her until she couldn't be seen. For the next hour, he swam in the ocean to calm the sexual urges trying to control him. After he tired himself out, he felt like napping as well and walked back to his room. For the time being, he was happy that he and Odette were together again, even if it were in separate places.

Odette's nap didn't last long, erotic dreams woke her up. She'd been panting and calling out for Griffin. Sitting up in bed, she flipped on the television to idly pass the time, and while she sat mindlessly watching the screen, she talked with Zion, "Thanks for clearing my head this morning. If you hadn't we'd probably still be having sex on the beach. Griffin is more handsome than I remembered. I hated I had to leave him, but I had to sleep, but I can't. My libido in on overdrive. Even in my dreams, I crave him. How will I get through the evening, without breaking down?"

"It won't be easy, but it will be worth your effort, "Zion replied.

Odette confesses, "I may need a chaperone. Can you linger in the shadows somewhere and keep me focused?"

"Now, you want me looking over your shoulder? What a sweet request. Odette, I will be close by, but you must do all this by yourself. I know you can do this, just don't bait him," Zion said.

"What do you mean by baiting him? Should I dress frumpy, wear no make-up, and revert back to looking like a spinster?" Odette asks.

Zion sighs, "No, dear. Dress nicely, use make-up, and do your hair. You will make Griffin's mouth water without purposely doing something provocative or lude. Enjoy the evening, just don't touch him inappropriately then expect him to have control. That's not fair if your plan is to know each other's likes and dislikes instead of sexual needs."

Odette understood what Zion meant. It didn't take much to ignite Griffin's passions and it wouldn't be fair to expect him to calm the need. So, she focused on dressing nice but not seductive and didn't overplay the make-up.

Choosing a yellow sundress that didn't show much skin, and a pair of flat sandals, she felt like a teenager again; innocent and sweet for her first date.

Griffin was clean, shaven, in his new outfit and out his door at 6:00 p.m. He planned to run in Wal-Mart and grabbed a bouquet of flowers for Odette. He wanted to make a good impression. After his purchase, he arrived at Odette's condominium precisely at 6:30 p.m., and he didn't have to wait for her to show up.

The sight of her made Griffin's heart pound. She was lovely to look at. Not his porcelain dove anymore, she didn't even look like a fairy princess either. She was a tanned goddess, standing strong in front of the building, looking beautiful in a yellow colored dress, with her pretty lips dyed a dark peach tint, Taking in all of her appearances, Griffin also noticed that her hair wasn't the same bright red anymore, it had also changed colors and had streaks of gold shimmering in the sunlight from her lying in the sun for several days.

Griffin instantly noted that Odette was a new creation, his wife had changed, and he liked it. He respected her for wanting a new beginning. Now, everything was up to him to make her feel special. He was going to treat her like a queen in every way and gouge her for information about her life. He wasn't going to leave another detail unturned about her again. Griffin planned to unravel this puzzle who was eagerly waiting for her first date.

From Dusk to Dawn

Odette hadn't seen Griffin's truck before, so she was unaware of him driving into the parking lot. Her attention was on some children when he walked up to her with flowers in his hand.

"Hi, gorgeous. What has you smitten?" Griffin asked her.

Odette honestly replies, "children. Since I've been here I keep thinking about having kids one day."

Griffin didn't flinch at her statement. He handed her the flowers and said frankly, "I want kids too. I can hardly wait to have a little Indian princess with red hair.

Odette smiled and said, "I'm glad you want kids. It's something we never discussed before marriage. Thanks for the flowers, they are lovely. Would you mind following me to my room? I need to put them in some water, so they don't die? It won't take but a few minutes."

Her invitation to go to her room was out in the open before she realized what she had said, and Zion overheard her words and stirred up a breeze that flushed an empty plastic bottle out of the bushes at Odette's feet.

The wind didn't alert Odette of Zion's promise to be near, but the bottle slapping at her ankle did, and she stopped in mid-step and remembered what she'd been told about baiting. "Ah… Griffin, I have a better idea. There is a water fountain inside this office. If we cut the top off this bottle, it would make a vase for my flowers and we can take them with us. I want to enjoy them during the evening. Do you mind?"

Griffin didn't mind. He took the bottle from her hand and went to his truck for something to cut the plastic. In a few seconds, he had the bottle cut and was inside the office in search of water. Zion, spoke softly in his absence to Odette, "I promised to be close, but I will only do so much, Odette. You must be careful. Griffin is suffering sexually. He's trying is best to remain in control."

"I'll try. Thanks for the heads up. I really wasn't thinking," Odette confessed.

"Here's your water, Odette. We'll place the flowers in the back, so you can see them," Griffin stated after coming out of the office.

Griffin led Odette to his truck and opened the passenger door for her. She was impressed by his truck because it wasn't anything like his tiny, sparse apartment. The truck was new, with all the bells and whistles, plus it was spacious enough to have some medical equipment in the back seating area.

"Do you always come prepared for animal emergencies?" She asked Griffin.

He realized she was trying to gather information about him, so he answered her completely, "Most of my business was out of the office. I majored in large animal care and minored in the small. Before I met you, I spent just about all my time working. I'd visit ranches in the morning and then practice small animal care after lunch. My days were full until I hired two other vets to help me. I practically lived at the clinic."

"That explains a lot. Your apartment wasn't… homey," she thoughtfully said trying not to offend.

Her attempt at being kind intrigued Griffin and made him laugh, "I'm a minimalist when it comes to home décor. I don't need much, just the basics. If I'm honest, my office was more comfortable than my apartment. I'm sad that I didn't get to show you my work environment. You would have been impressed."

Changing the subject, Odette said, "Let's eat at Uncle Ernie's Restaurant. Nathan said they have a killer seafood platter."

Griffin agreed and located the address through his Google app then he programmed his GPS, so they could find the restaurant easily. The traffic coming and going over Hathway Bridge was horrible, every few seconds they were stopped for some reason.

To lighten things up while they drove, Odette said, "traffic is the only drawback of being at this beach during the summer."

"Is traffic like this just during the summer or does this happen all the time? I'd go crazy if it was," Griffin replied.

Odette counters, "I've been here longer and had time to adjust. I asked around after a few times driving over the bridge when traffic was like this, and the people who live here said it is only bad a few months. They say it's especially bad on Saturdays because tourist are coming to the beach and others are leaving. Tourism is what the residents here rely on for their bread and butter. I'm glad I don't have to rely on someone's visit for my income."

Odette's comment interested Griffin. He felt Jesus was somehow responsible for the open door to ask a sensitive subject about relocation. Griffin gently approaches the subject with Odette, "do you like living in Georgia, Odette?"

Odette answered truthfully, "no not really. My parents are the only reason I moved back to Albany after college. When we married, my mind was set on being happy where you were. Happiness is a state of mind it doesn't come from outside forces, Griffin. What prompted you to ask?

"When I was in Albany searching for you, it occurred to me that you have a steady life in that area. Since I didn't have a business to hold me in Oklahoma, it made me think about moving there for you. I wanted you to be happy, Odette. But, I see now that you adjusted to me first. I appreciate that more than I can say," Griffin exclaimed.

"What about your mother? Shouldn't you be with her?" Odette quickly asked.

Griffin shrugged his shoulders and answered, "all my life, Mom depended more on my Uncle Randy than me. I was just the money-maker. She doesn't have to worry about money any longer. She'd adjust to me not being nearby. I think our relationship may improve if I wasn't around. Absence does make the heart grow fonder, I've heard."

Arriving at the restaurant, they shelved that conversation for another time, so they could focus on enjoying a good meal. Uncle Ernie's was a lovely place to eat and they thoroughly enjoyed their meal, but the historic part of Panama City is what really captured Odette's attention. Since it was no longer daylight, she made Griffin promise to return with her the next day, so she could feast on the town's history.

It was almost 10:00 p.m. by the time they found Club LaVela so they could dance. Instead of fighting the crowds, they both decided to search for Schooners. LaVela was too busy plus they felt overdressed.

When they went inside Schooners, they both agreed at first glance it had more of a laid-back feel and was the perfect place for Odette to have her first dancing experience. They were able to hear each other talk and enjoy a romantic evening.

They danced for hours and had a few too many drinks. Odette admitted loudly during a slow dance that she loved how it felt to sway in Griffin's arms. He realized she was not used to the effects of alcohol on sensual urges when she pleaded, "Griffin, can we go outside the club and sit on their porch for a while? I need to sober up some and cool off."

He said, "I know what you mean. I'm having difficulty myself. Dancing with you so close is raising my blood pressure. We both need a break."

Odette walked back to their table and gathered her handbag then headed for the porch. Griffin waved down a waiter and asked for two cups of very strong coffee before following her outdoors. They learned a lot about each other on that porch. The discussed silly things such as what their favorite foods were, favorite colors, and even divulged their dislikes. By 4:30 a.m. the waiters asked them to leave. Laughing on the way out to the truck, they realized they were sober enough for Griffin to drive them back to their condominiums.

They kissed passionately inside the truck for a few minutes until their bodies cried out for more. It was Griffin who made the first move this time and said, "I need some air and you need sleep."

He walked around to Odette's door and helped her out of his truck. Then he leaned inside and found the flowers in their plastic bottled and gave them to her. Odette started to walk away, but Griffin stopped her short, "Give me your cell number before you leave. I will never be without a way to talk to you ever again."

They logged each other's cell numbers in their phones and embraced but did not kiss. They ended the date the way it was supposed to end, each knowing more about the other and not just sexually. By the time they were relaxed enough to sleep in their separate condominiums, it was dawn.

Important Decision

While Odette and Griffin slept, Zion confronted Abba. "Will you tell me why are we are forcing these to people to stay away from each other? I know they had the cart before the horse a few weeks back, but they've made up and they had a successful evening that didn't involve a sexual romp. What more do you want?"

"They won't have to resist their natural urges much longer. I need them to see something first," Abba replied.

Zion crosses her arms and glared at Him, "What things? Why are you keeping me in the dark?"

Giggling at His bride, Abba reaches for her and pulls her close, "What's most important to us? What is the thing two people must discuss, before getting married?

Zion kisses Abba's cheek and hugs-Him tight before answering the question, "we want to raise their children. Odette and Griffin must agree on how they want us to inspire their babies!"

"They need a place of worship. I want them in one of our house with other believers as often as possible, so their children will grow up knowing our loving nature. Otherwise, their union will be like sinking sand, or a house made of straw trying to battle strong winds. Friends and family who support each other like Jesus taught can help them weather the storms that will happen." Abba states.

Out of concern, Zion inquires, "Finding a place of worship is important, but Griffin has never had that kind of lifestyle or other people to pray with. What should Jesus and I do to guide them in the right direction? Both love this beach. Should we lead them to one of our churches here?"

"Two generations ago, with Odette's grandmother and Chad Clearwater, heaven tried to bring peace between two cultures without my involvement, and it failed. Back then, Chad was unwilling to learn our ways from Odette's grandmother and when their parents confronted them, he didn't have our protection to lean on. Griffin does. When the time came for Odette and Griffin to meet, I made sure the same error didn't happen with them. I insisted you be involved with their union. Both Odette and Griffin were introduced to you, and because of you, Griffin was willing to follow Jesus. You weren't there for Chad. When Griffin needed you, you were the one who gave him clues to follow Jesus, remember?

You see, it doesn't matter where they find a church home, but wouldn't it be wonderful if we healed an old wound in the process? Panama City is a special place for Odette's grandmother, now it is special to Odette and Griffin. Odette's grandmother will feel special knowing she helped her granddaughter find happiness. We have everything in place, so have fun finding our two love-birds a home so they can be with others like themselves," Abba urges.

After their discussion, Zion got busy. Odette needed to know why her mother helped Griffin find her.

Odette's cell phone forced her from sleep. The call was from her mother. "Hello, dear. How are you?"

Even in her sleepy state, Odette knew why her mother called. "I'm fine, Mom. Griffin and I had a late night out and I was sleeping in."

"Alone?" Her mother curiously asked.

Odette quips, "Yes, alone. We are working out our issues. I'm making sure he loves me this time."

"Did he tell you why I gave him your address?" Her mother asked.

"No, Mom, that wasn't discussed. Why did you?" Odette inquired.

Her mother replies, "Griffin touched my heart. He showed me the two golden charms Grandma gave you and asked me if they were family heirlooms. When I asked how he got them, he said you lost them in his apartment the day you two wed.

I told him they were special to our family because of what they represented. His statement after I said Jesus was our anchor and cornerstone for a living, made me think differently about him. He said you had led him to Christ. Is that true?"

"Yes, it's true. Griffin and I know Christ personally," Odette confessed.

"Then the two of you shouldn't have much more to discuss. I know Griffin loves you and you love him. Trust in your Savior to make your marriage work. Set down roots and flourish," her mother advised.

When the two women finished their conversations, Odette rolled over and stared at the ceiling. She'd been a fool to worry about her future with Griffin, so she picked up her cell phone and made the next move to communicate with her husband.

Griffin's ringing cell phone jarred him awake. "Hello," he answered.

"It's time you kept your promise," Odette tells him.

Griffin asks, "what promise?"

"You promised to take me back to the old historic area of St. Andrews. I don't want to waste my day in bed. Get up and come get me," Odette demanded.

"Okay, okay. Give me thirty minutes to force down some coffee and dress. Meet me out front again," Griffin said.

Thirty minutes wasn't long enough for Odette to primp like she wanted, so she settled for comfort and simplicity. After quickly showering she threw on shorts and a tank top, put her hair in a ponytail without putting on make-up. In her mind, Griffin had seen her looking far worse, so he wouldn't care how she looked.

Griffin showered and dressed quickly as well, his stomach growled but he didn't take time to eat, instead, he settled for coffee and even drank it on the way to pick up Odette. As soon as he stepped out of the truck, Odette asks, "I'm hungry, are you?"

Griffin smiles, "Yes, I'm hungry. My stomach has been growling, it thinks my throat's been cut."

They got a fast food meal and drove back to the St. Andrews area, so they could look around the quaint historic part of Panama City. The first thing that grabbed Odette's attention was a huge Farmer's Market on the street they traveled along the bay. Odette begged to look around because she loved to scout through markets. At home, she liked to visit the town's outdoor market to buy her fruit and vegetables during the summer.

Griffin enjoyed walking around the market with her. More than anything, he loved seeing his wife in a different light. She was more than a beautiful woman, he noticed by the way she studied the local produce that she must like to cook and that was something he didn't know before.

"If I buy some food will you cook for me?" Griffin asked her.

She didn't hesitate, "you read my mind. I want to cook for you. I planned to ask you to dinner at my place. Help me pick something we would both enjoy eating.

They purchased all kinds of local produce because both of them liked fresh vegetables. Before they left, they met a honey harvester who was selling his local honey and had a lovely conversation with him. Griffin even asked him about his farm.

Zion and Jesus were working hard to guide them in the right direction. When the beekeeper said he wasn't the only farmer in the area it made Griffin ask if there were livestock farms around. When the old gentleman said there were several, it gave him something to ponder.

While they walked around the Marina, Griffin stops Odette and asks, "would you like living in Panama City with me?"

Odette asked a question, "you'd give up your practice to move here?"

He confidently answered, "what practice, it's in rubbles, remember. I'm waiting for the insurance money to rebuild. I don't see why I can't build something here. Until I get the money to build or find a place to work, I can work from my truck, I'll visit the livestock owners the beekeeper told me about and establish a reputation as a Veterinarian with them. Starting over won't be too hard, I have skills and can talk shop."

Odette answers, "I can look for a job teaching here also. If I can't find anything I can sub my teaching skills out online or tutor kids until something opens for me. I don't think I want to live on the beach, though. I like this historic part of town better. The beach is more recreational and wouldn't be a good place to raise a family in my opinion."

"I agree. I'd like to look around the bay area for a house. I don't want to live in another apartment. I like it here," Griffin stated.

Odette remembers what her mother said about establishing roots, and blurts, "if you are sure, then I'm all in, I'd love a home, but first we need to find a good place to worship. That's important to me."

Griffin looked at her puzzled for a few seconds, then he slaps his forehead, "Duh! I hadn't thought of that. We can ask around while we are here. Local people would know more about the churches in this area. I agree with you. We must start our married life right."

Odette grins, "I hoped you'd agree with me. Mom said you told her you were following Christ."

"You spoke to your Mom about me?" Griffin asked.

"Yes, she woke me up this morning. I knew why she'd called, the moment I saw her name on my phone. It wasn't hard to figure out after you told me she gave you my address. She also said you had my charms and asked about them. You made a good impression on her, Griffin, now let's stay on course and anchor our lives with together Jesus. It'd make my family proud to know we wanted to be part of a Christian environment with other believers," Odette replied.

Searching For Homes

Walking back to the truck, they noticed a small coffee shop on the street corner next to the Farmer's Market. They were unaware they were being supernaturally guided to a specific area. Because they were thirsty, they went inside to order an iced coffee and a snack. The owner of the shop was very friendly while he served them and kept engaging them in conversation. This made it easy for Griffin and Odette to ask him a few questions since the guy loved to talk.

Griffin asked him, "can you recommend a church in this area that caters to a younger crowd? My wife wants to find a place with people our age, so we can make friends and not just filled with white-haired people who are set in their ways."

The shop owner was happy to tell them about NorthStar Church. He said he attended their services as much as he could and enjoyed the atmosphere and it was full of people their age. When he explained that the church was so large the pastor had to give two sermons on Sunday mornings and evenings, it really interested Odette.

Odette asked him about a dress code and she was told it was a very informal place, and that most people wore shorts during the summer months Then she asked what time the services started. When he said the first service on Sunday evenings began at 5:30 p.m., so parents with small children could worship and be home early, she looked at Griffin and said, "we have time to visit and make it back to my apartment in time for me to cook a quick meal. Do you want to visit? This church sounds great!"

"Sure, but we have a few hours until then what do you want to do?" He asked her.

Odette asks the guy, "are there any houses for sale along the bay? We're considering relocation."

The guy informed them that the bay area had several lovely homes facing the water on West Beach Drive, and he gave Griffin clear instruction to follow. Before they left his shop, he also wrote down the address to NorthStar Church for them.

West Beach Drive was a beautiful street. It faced the bay and had low hanging trees branches shading the street, but they didn't block the view of the water. Odette loved the area instantly, and it wasn't long before they found a house for sale that they loved from the outside.

The house wasn't empty, so they couldn't look inside. Without disturbing the family inside, Griffin retrieved a flyer from a box next to their mailbox that belonged to a real estate firm. The flyer had all the necessary information about the house. They couldn't believe how fast their plan was manifesting but decided everything depended on them finding a good church home first.

At first glance, Odette loved NorthStar. It reminded her of the church she attended when she went to college. From every direction, she noticed teenagers and young adults flocking inside the doors, but she wasn't certain it was their church home until hearing the pastor preach. Everything he said during the service was on target with what she believed.

The music captivated Griffin. He'd never heard songs of that nature before. They had him very emotional before the pastor began his message. Just as Jesus and Zion planned, Griffin's heart was ready to receive a loving message that would make him a great father.

After the service, while they drove back to Odette's condominium, Griffin confessed that he had never experienced anything like that service. Odette agreed and said she wanted to return for a Wednesday night's service, to see what it was like before deciding it was their new church home. She explained that a mid-week service usually showed who the true believers really were. If a younger crowd returned she would know.

Griffin's truck wasn't registered with the Long Beach Resort, so they had to park in the office parking lot instead of inside the gates. Odette explained to the desk clerk that Griffin was her visitor and his truck wouldn't stay there overnight. Afterward, they unloaded the groceries and went to Odette's condominium.

While Odette prepared their meal, Griffin noticed a Bible on a table and picked it up and started flipping through the pages. "I need to buy one of these for myself, so I can learn more," he said.

Odette commented, "a Bible is a good start, but it's not God's complete truth. There are too many interpretations of it and people have gotten His true meanings confused. You'll need to seek the Holy Spirit's advice daily, so you can find the truth for yourself. Jesus taught me that.

That's how I knew what to listen for at tonight's service, I asked the Holy Spirit to help me discern His ways before the service started. If the pastor had preached anything other than love and acceptance, I wouldn't want to return. God's Holy Spirit is what completes a loving environment and teaches you correctly. Without Him, things fall apart because they are man inspired instead of God inspired."

Griffin looked at her confused, then asked, "I don't understand, I thought Jesus was all we needed. Can you show me in this book what you mean?"

Odette walked out of the kitchen and retrieved another Bible. It was a different version than the one Griffin held. While she watches over her cooking, she directed him to certain books inside their Bibles to get her point across the same way Jesus showed her. She asked Griffin to find the book of Galatians in the one he held and go to chapter 5. Then she told him to find verse 22 and asked him to read it from her Grandma's New American Standard version.

Griffin began to read aloud, "*But the fruit of the Spirit is love, joy, peace, patience, kindness, goodness, faithfulness, gentleness, self-control, against such things, there is no law.*"

When Griffin finished she asked him to read the same scriptures from her Bible. *But what happens when we live God's way? He brings gifts into our lives, much the same way that fruit appears in an orchard—things like affection for others, exuberance about life, serenity. We develop a willingness to stick with things, a sense of compassion in the heart, and a conviction that a basic holiness permeates things and people. We find ourselves involved in loyal commitments, not needing to force our way in life, able to marshal and direct our energies wisely.*

Legalism is helpless in bringing this about; it only gets in the way. Among those who belong to Christ, everything connected with getting our own way and mindlessly responding to what everyone else calls necessities is killed off for good—crucified.

After he finished reading the passage, Odette asked, "Do you see what I mean? The two books say basically the same thing only in different ways. The first Bible explains what God's spirit produces when we act under the guidance of Jesus. The other Bible you read, explains it in a manner you may understand better. It explained God's spirit in natures terms. Both are true. Does this help you see what I mean about misconceptions forming without proper guidance?"

"What if the pastor at NorthStar talked about legalism, would you want to listen further, in hopes he changes tunes?

Odette blurts, "Nope! I asked for guidance. I expected God's spirit to answer. If the pastor had talked about the Ten Commandments, I would have known I was in the wrong place. Like both verses in Galatians said, rules and regulations do not bring about a peaceful existence. Jesus fulfilled the law. We live totally by grace now."

Griffin admitted he had a lot to learn and that he was happy he had her to help him understand.

During their dinner, Griffin approached Odette with another idea, "as soon as I'm allowed to live with you again, we must find our own place to stay until we have a house. These condominiums are expensive. I said I didn't want to live in an apartment, but I will for a short time if we don't find something quickly."

Griffin's statement made Odette think, and she came to terms with her hurt feelings. Their two days together had proved to her that she loved Griffin inside and out and it was time to be a proper spouse. "We don't have to move," she confessed.

"Why? Isn't this place costing you a small fortune? I didn't think teachers made that kind of money," he commented.

She clears things up, "my salary has nothing to do with renting this place, Griffin. My Grandpa owns it and has loaned it to me for as long as I need. We can stay here, rent free, until October. That's when Grandpa wants to rent the condominium to people he calls snowbirds who are seeking warmer climates during the winter."

"Does that mean I can move in?" He quickly asked.

Odette puts her elbows on the table, looks into Griffin's bright eyes and kindly said, "one more night apart, I need time to myself for a little longer."

"Can I ask why?" He inquired

"It has nothing to do with you, this time. What I mean is I need quiet time with Jesus. Some moments shouldn't be shared in front of another person. If you stayed the night, I'd be distracted, and I have a lot to thank Him for, Griffin," she explained.

Griffin replied, "I do too. I'll do the same."

It was late when they finished eating and they both were exhausted from everything they had done. If they were to spend time with Jesus, they had to make the time before going to sleep.

Before leaving Odette, Griffin explained that he would be checking out of the Majestic at 9:00 a.m. and she told him that she would meet him in the Long Beach Office so he could change his reservation to an ownership status, so he could move in with her rent-free.

Interruption

After Jesus met separately with each of them, He returned to Abba and Zon with news of their happiness. When He was finished sharing how they had thanked Him for their reunion, Abba had something to say, "then it's time to move things along faster."

Jesus asked, "what is your plan?"

"It is time for baby Waters to interrupt their plans and get mama and papa's attention. When they realized a baby is on the way, they won't waste time in the condominium having sex all the time. A baby's demands will take priority," Abba informed.

At 7:00 a.m., Griffin's phone rang. It was Odette. Answering he asked, "hi! What's up?"

Panting in the phone, Odette squeaked, "I'm sick, Griffin. Can you come now? I called the front office and asked that they allow you in before 9:00 a.m. I told them I was sick and needed my husband. They promised to have everything ready when you arrived. Come quick. I've been sick all night and I feel faint."

Griffin didn't take time to shower, and spent the time quickly packing and gathering the food he'd purchased. After checking out of his condominium, with each breath he took, he prayed, "Jesus, please be with Odette. Make sure she is okay."

When Griffin arrived at the Long Beach Resort, a lady unlocked the office and gave him a key and parking pass. He thanked her for coming in early and rushed up to check on Odette.

When he opened the condominium door, he called her name but heard no answer. He found her lying on the bathroom floor too weak to speak. Thankful for his medical training, Griffin gathered her up and placed her on the bed.

"Are you in pain?" He asks.

Odette shakes her head and softly said, "I've been vomiting all night. I'm too hot and the bathroom tile was cool, so I stayed there.

Griffin knew then why she was weak. He rushes to the kitchen and gets a cup of crushed ice from the refrigerator. When he returns to Odette, he helps her sit up on the bed and spoons ice into her mouth. "You're dehydrated, Odette, you need water. Suck on this ice and let's see if it stay down."

The ice helped Odette feel better, but when she tried to drink anything she couldn't keep it down. All Griffin managed was to feed her ice chips or help her in the bathroom. He made sure her hair was held back and her face was wiped with a cool washcloth while she got sick.

In the back of his mind, every time Odette vomited, he wondered if it was more than a stomach bug. When she began to feel better before lunch, his suspicions were peaked. He held the thoughts inside for later. He was happy she felt better.

Sipping on a glass of water and munching on dry toast, Odette asked, "Griffin, will you go across the street to Wal-Mart and buy something for an upset stomach?. I want something to take if I get sick after eating this toast."

Griffin rushed to Wal-Mart and purchased something Odette could use for nausea that she wouldn't have to swallow. He also picked up two pregnancy tests as well. If Odette was sick the next day, he would insist she uses them.

Their first day and night together under the same roof were spent in bed, but not the way they expected their new union to be. Griffin, watch television in bed, so he could stay near Odette while she slept. He wanted to make sure she was over the illness.

They ate scrambled eggs and toast for dinner on the balcony before going back to the bedroom. Everything seemed to be returning to normal, but sex was the last thing on Griffin's mind. All he wanted was for Odette to feel better.

They fell asleep in each other's arms while watching television, but around midnight, Griffin was startled out of sleep when Odette lost her dinner in the bathroom. This time, he was convinced she had more than a stomach virus. He rushed to the kitchen grabbed a cup of ice, the suppositories for nausea, and one of the pregnancy tests.

Returning to Odette with the tests behind his back, he explained, "Odette, you need more than Pepto Bismal to ease your nausea. I grabbed something else to for you to use."

Odette looked at the suppositories he gave her and hysterically said, "you're not watching me insert these. Go away!"

Before he closed the bathroom door, he handed her the pregnancy test that he'd held behind his back, "before you insert the suppository, do this test for me."

Odette's eyes went wild when she saw the pregnancy test in Griffin's hand. She squealed, "you think I'm pregnant?

"I'm almost sure of it, Odette. The signs are there, and the timing is right," he confesses while closing the bathroom door.

Five minutes later, Odette opened the door with the pregnancy test in her hand. She looked scared and she asked, "how'd this happen? We used precautions."

"It's positive, then?" Griffin excitedly asked.

Odette whispers, "yes, it's positive. Now what?"

Griffin helped Odette back to bed and sat on the edge beside her. He takes her hand and sweetly says, "during our sexual role-playing, the protection I used ruptured. I didn't tell you because I didn't want you to worry.

The morning it occurred, I asked myself several questions when I was alone in the bathroom, and I came to the conclusion I could not live without you. That's what prompted my request to marry. I'm ready to be a father. I knew it then. I want it even more now that we are back together. I pray you feel the same."

With tears streaming down her face, Odette admitted. "I've been dreaming about kids since my first day here at Panama City Beach. I loved watching small kids play on the beach. This makes me want to live here even more. I will get to see our kids play in the sand and water instead of watching others."

The first suppository eased Odette's nausea enough for her to get some rest. When she woke after a few hours, she was sick again, and she wasn't scared this time. Griffin had been right to buy something other than Pepto Bismal. She used the medicine, again, and quietly slid back into bed to relax next to her husband. She turned on her side and waited for the medicine to work while she watched him sleep. She felt blessed that Griffin had medical training, and could take care of their family when sicknesses occurred. At that point, she mentally thanked God for bringing her such a wonderful person to spend her life with.

When the sun began to shine through their bedroom window, Odette crawled out of bed and slid the balcony door open, so she could hear the ocean waves. It didn't take long for her to realize they had a lot to do. "Griffin, wake up! We can't waste time!"

He opened his eyes and asked, "are you sick again?"

She rattled out, "been there done that while you slept through my last episode. We have a lot to do. We're not daydreaming anymore. A baby is coming and we have no time to waste."

"Take a breath, Odette. We're financially secure enough to take our time," Griffin stated.

She vents, "that's not the issue, Griffin! I must give notice at school. We need to buy a house and move our things here. I'll need to go back to Albany and pack. Heaven knows how we'll get your things to Florida. I refuse to be separated again and I will not travel that far! Good Lord, we will have a baby in a few months and I will be left alone to manage this without you."

"Your hormones are working overtime, sweetheart. Slow down, we'll work things out step-by-step and we won't have to be separated to do all this," Griffin soothed.

Odette took a deep breath, and said, "I need a shower. The running water will clear my head."

Griffin made coffee, toast for Odette and scrambled a few eggs for himself while she showered. When she came to the kitchen she had a towel on her head and had thrown on shorts and a tank top. Her attempt to overcome morning sickness made Griffin smile.

"I made you some toast if you feel like eating. It might do you some good to sip on some coffee. Caffeine withdrawal will give you a headache on top of nausea," he informed.

She replied, "thanks! I'm very hungry. Hopefully, I can keep the toast down. It isn't fun having to stick something up my butt to keep from being sick."

Griffin laughed and poured two cups of coffee and took them to the balcony. Odette follows the divine smelling brew and waits for Griffin to return with their breakfast. To her surprise, he brings her cell phone with him. "we have people to call. I don't want your mother angry with me for keeping our news from her," he joked

Odette takes her phone and jokes back, "you must call yours too. I'm sure I won't get her well wishes."

Griffin didn't reply to her pun, he knew what his mother would say. He'd prepared her for the news of a baby the day he and Odette married, but he went after his phone anyway to give her the good news.

After sipping on the coffee and biting into her toast, Odette phoned her mother and put the call on speaker, so Griffin could hear their conversation. When her mother answered, Odette softly states, "hi, Grandmama. Griffin and I are back together, plus one."

Her mother squills, "what did you call me? Say it ain't so? A baby, so soon?"

"Afraid so, Mom. I took a pregnancy test last night and it came back positive," Odette shared.

"Why? Do you have morning sickness?" Her mother asked her.

Odette said, "It's awful! If it wasn't for Griffin, I'd still be sick. He had sense enough to get me the right medicine to settle my stomach."

"I had morning sickness bad, too. Eat crackers and sip on Ginger Ale, they will help. Just don't get dehydrated," her mother urged.

. "I have been through that, too. Thank God, Griffin knew what I needed. He had me crunching on ice."

"Tell Griffin I knew I would fall in love with him," her mother joked.

"I fell in love with you, too," Griffin shouts into the air so Charlene could hear him on the other end of the phone.

Then, Odette says, before ending their call, "tell Dad and call Grandpa and Grandma to let them know we plan on staying a while longer. I'll call you again soon with more details. Love you."

After the call to Odette's mother, Griffin begged off from calling his. He didn't want to ruin their mood, and he explained this to Odette. She understood and didn't want to be unhappy either.

Griffin did place a call to someone, though. Odette heard him ask to speak with someone about the house they loved on West Beach Drive. She was happy he was taking things seriously and that nausea wasn't stopping their plans.

Going With the Flow

An appointment to see the house on West Beach Drive was made with the real estate agent for 2:00 p.m. They left the condominium early and to pass the time, they stopped and purchase saltine crackers and Ginger Ale for Odette along with a few cans of chicken noodle soup.

While they were in the grocery store, Griffin shared something Odette's mother said to him, "before I left your parents' house, your mother gave me some advice that I will never forget. She said to live in the flow of God's love and count on Him. To be content and patient. So, if this house isn't the one for us, I won't be disappointed. We'll find something better, I'm sure of this."

"That sound like something Mom would say. She and Dad are devout believers, it took longer to convince me that I needed a personal relationship with Jesus. I agree with them now. I still jump into fits of confusion from time to time, like I did with you this morning. You can help me stay in this flow," Odette shared.

Abba was amused by Griffin's 'rhythm of love' statement to Odette, it meant he expected things to go slowly for them and with obstacles. When He huffed, I wasn't surprised when He demanded a meeting with Jesus and I and expected us to instantly appear in the observation room that looked over His earthly realm.

We were sitting, when He began to speak, "I want you to understand that Griffin and Odette are not the main focus for me. I am on a mission to bring happiness back to Zion, using them. She's not felt like a creative being in a long while. To make this happen, I expect everything for Griffin and Odette to fall into place quickly. Zon must be involved in raising children again. Nothing, I mean nothing can hinder this. The Waters must become an established family in the place of their choosing and grounded by '*Jesus' kind of faith*' flowing through them, so they don't depend on their own efforts.

If they choose to buy a home in Florida, make it happen quickly and without issues. I don't like sloppiness."

Then Abba addresses Jesus directly, and demands, "always have your angels stationed in Oklahoma, Georgia, and Florida, ready to assist Griffin and Odette with their plans. Make their transitions simple, I want it known to this couple that I will bless them without placing tests and trials in front of everything they want to accomplish. Once they are settled and their baby is born, convince them to do what I want. Is this understood?"

"Yes, Abba, I completely understand, and I'd like to say I enjoy your input and guidance, it's a pleasure having you involved. Teamwork makes me feel more alive," Jesus exclaimed.

The real estate agent was waiting on Griffin and Odette when they pulled into the house's driveway. The three of them were alone inside the house, so Griffin felt comfortable asking questions. He even asked if a home inspection was provided before making an offer, which surprised Odette. She hadn't thought of something that crucial and was glad Griffin had taken control of the meeting.

When the agent showed Griffin a good inspection report on the house and explained that one had been ordered because another couple had wanted to buy the house and then backed out without warning. The owner's selling price almost made Odette faint, but Griffin did n't wince, balk, or complain. His composure impressed her, especially when he said, "give my wife and I a few hours to decide. We will call you soon."

It wasn't until they were in the truck that Odette attempted to speak clearly. She slowly said, "I know you said to go with the flow and not worry, but a two hundred seventy-five thousand dollars is a lot of money. I like the house, but is it worth that much?"

"I have a plan, Odette. Trust me," Griffin assured.

Griffin made a search on his phone for the Bay County Tax Accessors' Office, then he set his GPS to head that way. In the office, he explained to a clerk why he wanted to know the taxable amount of the property. The clerk took Griffin into another room and complied with his request while Odette waited. The taxable amount the county estimated on the property was a lot less than the owner's asking price. Griffin knew exactly how much to make an offer for the house after reading the report. He didn't say anything inside the building to Odette, but when they were inside his truck, again, he told her everything.

"Odette, the county estimates the house value at two hundred and ten thousand, we can handle that, maybe even a two hundred thirty. I refuse to pay what the owners want. I think they are expecting an unreasonable profit. Do you want to try my offers? It can't hurt to bid," Griffin said.

She replied, "sure! Let's give it a shot. If this isn't our house, I believe what you said, God has something better around the corner."

Griffin called the Real Estate agent and made the offer of two hundred and fifteen thousand as their first bid. Then he told the realtor if the owners balked then offer two hundred thirty thousand, but no more. The called ended, and the waiting game began for them to hear back from the owners.

Driving around town, Griffin noticed a shopping mall and commented that he was always hot and he needed clothes suitable for Florida weather. Odette agreed to shop even though she still didn't feel completely well. She knew Griffin needed cooler clothes, and he would be sensitive to her needs if she couldn't shop long.

It didn't take very long for Griffin to find a few items and as they headed out to the truck, a jewelry store caught his eye. "Odette, would you like a wedding band?" He asked.

Flabbergasted by his question, because it was totally unexpected, she truthfully answered, "yes I would. I think it's time I wore a ring that marks me as unavailable.

They chose two rings, a plain band for Griffin and a three-stone diamond band for Odette that Griffin purchased with a credit card. Before leaving the store, they placed the rings on each other's finger. The gesture made Odette cry with happiness.

Griffin pinches her chin and forces her to look into his eyes, "are you ready to resume where we left off almost a month ago. I've proven my love to you Can we go home, so I can show you I mean it, Mrs. Waters?" He asks.

Odette giggles with glee, and jokingly admitted, "if I can manage not to rape you in the truck before we can get there.

They make it back to the condominium. Griffin carried her over the threshold and shut the door with his foot then they immediately began undressing each other. The sex was intense but different than before. It was better because they didn't have to worry about using pregnancy prevention.

They spent hours making love and when they finished, Griffin leans over and placed his face on Odette's stomach and endeared himself to her again, "hi, little one. I'm your Daddy. Get used to hearing my voice because we will have a wonderful relationship. My job is to love you and Mom, and I plan to do that well."

Back in Oklahoma, they would relax in each other's arms after sex, until they grew hungry enough to order room service, but this time Griffin didn't lie in bed, he threw his jeans back on and warmed up some soup for Odette. He didn't want her to refuse food.

Odette was afraid to eat even though she was hungry. To appease Griffin, though, she threw on a robe and met him on the balcony where she slowly ate her soup while he scarfed down a couple of sandwiches. Odette pinched her nose and couldn't finish the soup, so Griffin ran and poured her a glass of Ginger Ale to soothe her quivering tummy. He resumed eating the sandwich until she fled to the bathroom

"The Ginger Ale didn't help?" He asked.

She admitted, "I don't think I drank enough for it to work. It was the garlic smell coming from the sandwich meat you were eating that turned my stomach. The soup wasn't the issue."

Remembering what his mother-in-law said, Griffin calmed his emotions and helped Odette back to the balcony and brought her another bowl of soup. He finished his meal in the kitchen and brushed his teeth afterward, so she wouldn't smell the garlic on his breath when he returned.

"Did you manage to eat a few spoons full of soup?" He asked.

"I ate a noodle or two," she joked.

Speaking with a concerned voice, instead of jokingly responding back to her, Griffin said, "I'll be honest, Odette, I want to rush you to the hospital, but I realize this sickness is part of pregnancy, and I need to stay calm and be patient, so I can trust the flow. But, if you can't keep nourishment in your system, soon, I will insist that you be given an intravenous supplement. Do you understand? I'm not joking about this, okay?

Overwhelmed by Griffin's concern for her, Odette mentally cried out to Zion for help before agreeing with her husband. Then she said, "yes, Doctor Waters, I understand your concern. I promise I will try and eat."

Odette's heartfelt cry for help moved Zion. She didn't hesitate to manifest, in her human form in front of them. "I'm here now, Odette. How can I help?"

Unbelievable Fast Pace

Griffin didn't give Odette a chance to answer Zion, he blurted out his concerns right away. "She's starving. She can't live without fluids and food much longer, neither can the baby. Help her!"

Zion sweetly answered, Griffin, "I understand the condition. I've been watching Odette struggle. It seems to occur during certain times of the night instead of the day. May I suggest you track the times the onsets happen? When you find moments that she isn't nauseated, then you can give her food and drink in between the attacks. Also, take notice of things that trigger her episodes. This last bout was due to a strong pungent smell."

Odette protests, "Hey, you two. I'm in the room, and I can hear. It's my body you are discussing. May I please ask questions?"

Griffin says, "sorry, Odette."

Zion asked, Odette, "are you hungry?"

Odette replied, "yes! The warm soup was good, and I was beginning to eat more of it until I smelled the garlic in Griffin's sandwich. Usually, I like spicy or seasoned foods, but the garlic was too strong, and it made the soup change taste in my mouth. It tasted like I was just eating garlic and it made my stomach flip."

"Do you feel sick now?" Zion asked.

Odette answered, "a little, but I don't want to eat the soup anymore."

Nibble on the crackers and sip the Ginger Ale. Extremely bland foods, such as dry toast and crackers, may be the only way you can function for a few weeks. Then slowly add good foods," Zion explained.

Griffin asked, "what should I buy for her?"

"Wean her off coffee with caffeine immediately. When she can eat, bake, or boil the meats she wants to eat. Don't fry anything, and use only salt. Add no other seasonings. Load her up with vegetables, nuts, and fruit as much as possible. She can eat baked potatoes, oatmeal and grains mixed with honey and fruit, without butter, and stay away from processed foods and sugars. Focus only on foods straight from nature, drink a lot of water, and get fresh air and sunshine," Zion instructed.

After giving them advice, Zion assured the couple she would always be near if they had questions, but she didn't want to intrude on their time alone. Throwing them a kiss, she disappeared.

After our meeting with Abba, we didn't waste any time with details. While Zion watches over Odette and Griffin, my job was to take notes so I could keep their story straight. Abba wants me to share their love story throughout the generations as an entertaining guide to true happiness.

Jesus' job is more intense because He and the angels must be involved in all the transitions this couple have to face.

It will take observing and investigations on every situation, even traveling through various time frames will be required, so they can make adjustments with the information they gather. Abba's demands on us were clear, He did not want rough edges or loose ends to correct.

Like clockwork, Odette's nausea returned after midnight, but all she did was dry-heave and spit out the taste of bile. When she felt better, she rinsed her mouth with mouthwash and the taste of it made her heave, again. She grabbed one of the suppositories and forced herself to use it. She gathered the strength to keep her promise to Griffin. She would pour herself a glass of Ginger Ale to sip on during the night.

She opened the bathroom door to go to the kitchen but didn't have to go far. Griffin was awake and standing outside the door with her some Ginger Ale and crackers. She took his offering and sat on the bed so she could eat as he watched.

"I hate my nausea wakes you up," she confessed.

Griffin smiled, and said, "we're in this together, remember, we are one person bound together forever. That's why couples claim 'they' are pregnant.

Odette nibbled more of the saltine crackers while Griffin massaged her shoulders. When it appeared she wouldn't heave again, they crawled back in bed and cuddled with him. Odette commented, "we can't act like newlyweds. We've only made love once since you move in with me."

"That must be a hint, Mrs. Waters? I'll tell you a secret, I'm always on ready when I'm near you. I was waiting for you to ask," Griffin admitted while removing her nightgown.

When Griffin woke, Odette was still asleep. Apparently, their passionate exercise had helped her. He rose quietly and headed towards the kitchen for a cup of coffee and remembered Odette shouldn't have much. So, he added ice to the hot brew and to quickly drink his two cups before showering. When he left the bathroom, Odette was awake and had a coffee mug in hand. It looked like she couldn't resist coffee. Griffin said, "take it easy. Zion said that was the first thing that had to go. I drank mine earlier not to tempt you."

Odette assured him, "for some uncanny reason, I didn't want coffee. I warmed some Ginger Ale in the microwave. It's good this way."

Their plan was to lounge in the sunshine and rest that morning, but it was raining outside when they dressed. Before Griffin had a chance to complain, an angel urged him to do some research. "Odette, did I see an iPad on your dresser?"

"I have a Kindle, it's not an iPad, why?" She asked.

Griffin replied, "it just occurred to me that we can do a lot of research online if we had a computer. We can look for jobs, do banking transactions and not have to travel. Anywhere. I'll rush to Wal-Mart and buy us one. While I'm away, call the front office and ask if they have a more secure Wi-Fi connection for owners."

Thrilled with Griffin's idea, she did as he asked as soon as he walked out of the condominium. The resort had a very secure access for condominium owners when they visited, and they only charged a small fee to use. She paid for the service of the phone and asked for a code.

Griffin was on his way back to the condominium with a new computer. He also had other software to install when his cell phone rang. It was the Real Estate Agent with the news. Their offer of two hundred thirty thousand dollars was accepted, but with one drawback, the owners asked if they could have until the end of August to move out. Griffin quickly assured him the August deadline would not be a problem.

Griffin had a huge smile on his face when he entered the condominium. When Odette asked why, he put the boxes down and scooped her up in his arms, and said, "we got the house! It's ours the end of August."

"That's only a few weeks away! Get that computer hooked up. We need to get busy," Odette said.

As soon as the computer was connected to electricity and programs downloaded, Odette entered the code to their secure Wi-Fi. Then like magic, they were ready to work. Odette had her passwords to a lot of sites, she used an app to keep the codes handy on her phone for quick use.

When she logged into her Facebook account she shouted at Griffin, "you sent me a friend request?"

He said, "it's the only social media account I remembered how to use. I reached out to you in desperation before I met your parents. I don't remember any of my other accounts accept my email and the one I use for my bank account, so I can pay bills. I hadn't wanted anything else. Lucy had programmed all the social media and business accounts on the computers back in Oklahoma."

Remembering how Lucy worked on his clinic computers gave him another idea, and he called his old secretary. When Lucy answered his call, he said, "hi, Lucy do you have time to work for me?"

"Is it full-time work or temporary? I can't risk losing unemployment if it is temporary, Griffin" Lucy explained.

"It's temporary, so I'll send Johnson the money. You won't have issues," Griffin answered.

"What do you need, then. We can really use the money," Lucy replied.

"Get a notepad, and come back to the phone I have a list," he said.

When she returned, he began, "write down all the identifications and passwords you used to set up my computers at the clinic and then email them to me. I will call you back in a few days when I have permission for you to enter my apartment and the clinic area"

"Why?" Lucy asked.

I need you to have someone pack up everything from both places and store all of my belongings in moveable storage pods. I'm moving and they'll need to be in transportable containers. We'll schedule them to arrive at 215 W. Beach Drive, Panama City, Florida the first week of September."

"You still haven't told me why you're moving, Griffin," Lucy insisted.

Griffin said, "my wife and I are not returning to Oklahoma, I bought a house here in Panama City, Florida. Odette and I want to start our marriage over in a new place.

"Does your mother know?" She asked.

Growling, he said, "not yet. I will tell her soon. Keep this secret unless she threatens your life."

"You got it, Griffin. Locked lips, I promise," Lucy assured him.

As soon as Griffin had an email from Lucy with the Id's and passwords, he showed them to Odette and she jotted them down in her app. Then he called Joe Stanley, the associate who told him about the computer cloud and asked him to teach Odette how to retrieve his business information.

With Joe's help, Odette managed to get everything Griffin needed on their new computer and then she politely ended the call with him. When Griffin saw what Lucy had created for his business, he shouted, "thank you, Jesus!"

Lucy hadn't wasted her skills. There were files listing everything; business banking information, medicine and other supplies, clients, phone numbers, addresses, as well as accounts receivables, listing who owed Griffin money. She even created a file to keep pictures of his business license and college diploma on hand.

To their surprise, by noon on that rainy day, they were almost halfway done with their transitioning to Florida. Griffin was excited and said, "we've done enough for the day. Let's work up an appetite for some lunch, are you game?"

Wednesday Night Insights

Griffin ate his lunch in the kitchen away from Odette, so she could enjoy her dry toast and noodle soup in the bedroom. Afterward, he insisted she take a nap, so she would feel like visiting NorthStar Church's Wednesday night service.

The rain had stopped, and the temperature was nice outside when they left the condominium. Griffin was familiar with the trek, but he still had problems patiently dealing with the tourism traffic along the beach and over Hathaway Bridge. When they arrived at the church, the service was underway, and he hated coming into any meeting late because people stared. Ironically, making them late was part of our plan.

Church visitors were always welcome at NorthStar, so when Griffin and Odette walked in late, the regular attendees knew instantly they had new people to engage.

It didn't surprise Odette when the Wednesday message was more geared towards members. The pastor talked more about the church's community missions than talking about Jesus' walk on earth. It impressed her when he referred to certain kinds of issues such as homelessness, addictive behaviors, domestic violence situations, and child care for single parents. What attracted her most, was when he said they were to be the arms and feet of Jesus so they could make life better for their community.

Griffin couldn't fully understand why people would want to actively get involved in handling another person's affairs, especially those involving addictive behaviors, like his Uncle Randy's. It bothered him that he might have to deal with drunks. and pretend to like it and not to offend anyone. He didn't shut down but listened to all of the pastor's message with a plan to discuss the issues with Odette when they returned home.

He did agree that the pastor's message tied in with the same scripture Odette showed in hin the condominium, but he wanted a deeper clarification about mission work. He also knew he must discuss his deep emotional wounds with Jesus, so resentments wouldn't keep raising their ugly head. It made him sad to think his Uncle Randy's treatment of him was still a touchy issue.

When the church service ended, people began to gather around them for introductions. One nice couple, Fred, and Glenda Harper, who was around their age, and lived in Panama City, invited them to have dinner with them at a restaurant up the street.

Griffin hesitated to answer them, he worried Odette wouldn't be able to tolerate the smells inside the restaurant, but when she excitedly chirped up he agreed to join them. On the drive to the restaurant, Griffin asked if she were well enough to eat and she informed him that she planned to nibble crackers so he could eat a good meal. When he protested, she shushed him and said it wasn't fair he had to eat sandwiches.

The seafood restaurant was in the historic district, and the Harpers assured them the food was excellent. After finding an empty booth, Odette explained why she wouldn't be eating and encouraged them to recommend good things to Griffin. He ordered cheese sticks as an appetizer and fried shrimp with French fries, and coleslaw for dinner. Odette ordered Ginger Ale and a basket of saltine crackers. The Harpers wanted raw oysters as their appetizer and a seafood platter with grits instead of fries to split between them.

Griffin glanced at Odette when the waiter brought the oysters to their table. He was surprised she didn't get sick because of the way they looked. /Raw oysters were new to him, and he couldn't understand how something that looked like snot would be good to eat. The sight unsettled him. Odette managed to eat crackers and sip her drink, but he couldn't watch the Harpers swallow the slimy things. He had to keep his head down not to be grossed out while he ate cheese sticks. His reaction to their food made him sympathize with Odette's condition even more.

When the oyster shells were removed from the table, Griffin was able to engage more in conversation. Odette excitedly told them about her pregnancy and their plan to move to Panama City. He got to say they liked NorthStar Church.

Glenda said, "in my opinion, you visited the best church in town. I hope you'll make it your church home. Fred and I get involved. He enjoys helping the needy and assisting the elderly. I like tutoring children when they get out of school"

Odette chimed in, "I'm a teacher, I'd like to tutor the kids after school until our baby gets older. It would give me something to do until I found somewhere to teach full time.

Fred asked, "What's your major, Odette. I can put in a good word for you at church."

"I have a doctorate in American History," she answered.

Glenda sputtered, "you're way too qualified to tutor in the after-school program. There is a new museum here on Beck Street that may need help. I feel that would be more interesting to you, plus you'd get paid. Tutoring at church is volunteer work."

Fred asked, "what line of work are you in, Griffin?

He answered, "I had an animal clinic back in Oklahoma, but my drunken Uncle set it on fire. I've put the property up for sale and will be seeking another Veterinarian.position here in Panama City."

Glenda commented, "meeting you guys was definitely a divine appointment! My Uncle is looking for someone to purchase his animal clinic in Lynn Haven. The business is located a few miles away from here. Can you prepare a resume or documents for us to show him?"

Griffin excitedly answered her, "sure, I can! I'll work up something for him tomorrow. I'll also provide farmers'names and numbers who would recommend me."

The two couple ended the night bonded in friendship, and made sure they exchanged numbers before going their separate ways. In the truck, Griffin said, "can you believe all that's happened for us today, Odette? Other than finding you, I've never been so fortunate."

Pulling out of the restaurant parking lot, Odette stated, "this is Beck Street, the same street we met the beekeeper and nice coffee shop owner. Glenda said the museum is on this street. I'd like to visit it tomorrow.?

Griffin replied, "if you want to be a stay at home mom with the baby I can take care of all of us. If this job pans out, we'll be established before the baby is due. That means a lot to me. I need to work, you don't have to."

Odette answered, "I don't want to stay at home all the time. I need some form of work to keep my mind busy. If I can find a part-time job that would be enough for me until our children were older."

"Does the museum appeal to you?" Griffin ask.

Odette admitted, "yes it does. I like to teach, but I love to study and research more. I should have extended my studies further into excavating historical sites."

"I can't picture you digging up old bones. I'm learning new things about you every day," Griffin stated.

Their conversation brought the treasures she found in Albany back into her mind and she said to Griffin, "I went digging in the Flint River a few months back and found some native artifacts. They helped fuel my desire to learn more about your culture. At first, I considered giving the bowl and utensils to a museum in town, but Zion forbids me. She said they were for my children, now I know why."

Griffin asked, "did you plan on marrying an Indian when you came to Oklahoma?"

"No, but I will confess, some native men light a fire in me. The first time I saw an Indigenous man dressed in native attire my body went into a sensual frenzy. I was at an Indian Festival at Chehaw Park when it happened. I saw many Indian men after that day, but the feelings didn't happen to me again until I saw you. When you were washing out my clothes in the stream, you looked good enough to eat."

He replied, "then I'm glad I have you all to myself and very far from other Indian men like me. I don't want to become a jealous man."

Returning To Albany

Some things can't be done online. Odette must take care of things in Albany and the time to do this was fast coming. Abba was pleased that within two weeks, we did arrange a lot, so they didn't have to travel much. We arranged for their bank accounts to be joined, their insurance information changed, and we helped them find jobs.

With the online assistance, they learned they each used banks that were also in other areas like Panama City that was an easy transition. Griffin's insurance just took a phone call to add Odette to his health plan all the necessary paperwork was handled through the internet.

Glenda's Uncle was very impressed with Griffin's credentials and everything he provided for him to inspect, but he had one request and that was for he and Griffin to work as a team for a few months, so he could ease out of the business and retire.

Odette and Griffin were dumbfounded when they visited the museum on Beck Street it was one that catered to Indigenous people. When she explained to the owner that she was looking for part-time work and had a doctorate degree in American History, he was interested, but when she explained to him that study and research was her passion, he asks if she would be willing to take a job helping him verifying objects as relics. When he said he would pay her well, she agreed that day to help him. Then gave him her phone number to call her when objects arrived.

Odette had to contact her current employer and resign. She also had to make arrangments with her apartment complex. The first thing she must do was legally change her name, and that meant she would need a birth certificate. They could have ordered one online, but they didn't have time to wait for it to arrive. Her name had to be Waters on a driver's license and Social Security Card before they could close on their new house in one week. That meant a visit to Albany was necessary.

The night before they were to go back to Albany, Odette called her Mom to give her the news that they were coming home. She explained to them several days before about their plans to move, so they were expecting them to return to pack her things. Because Odette wanted to bring back a few clothes from her apartment back to Florida, they drove her jeep instead of Griffin's truck and when her Dad saw the vehicle he greeted them as soon as they pulled into their driveway.

Odette's car door was opened by her Dad as soon as they stopped. He said, "let me see your belly. I can't believe I'm going to be a Granddaddy."

"Oh, Dad stop. I'm not showing yet. I can assure you though that I am pregnant," Odette says while giving him a hug.

He says to the two of them, "come in the house. Mom has planned a feast for all of us. Grandpa and Grandma will be here shortly, so they can meet Griffin."

Griffin and Odette followed Herman through the house into the kitchen where Charlene was cooking a large meal. When Charlene looked up from her visual at the stove, she saw who Herman had following him.

"Come here you two," she demanded.

Giving each of them a hug and kiss she then drew back and stared at Odette, then asked, "Have you been able to eat anything yet?"

Odette answered, "I've been living off saltines, dry toast, and noodle soup."

"I've cooked rice with the meal and I baked the chicken, in hopes you'd be able to eat with us," her mother said.

A shout from the living room made everyone take notice and Herman shouted back, "come in the kitchen, we're all in here."

My eyes were firmly set on Griffin. I was eager to see his expression when Odette's Grandmother came into view because Martha Hammond was an older version of her granddaughter.

Griffin's face exhibited shock. He turned to look at his wife, then at his mother-in-law and his movements caught Odette's attention. "Uncanny resemblance, isn't it?" Odette whispers up to him.

When Martha came closer to Odette and Griffin, she greeted her Granddaughter with a hug and kiss then reached up and touched Griffin's face and said, "you're just as handsome as Charlene's Dad. He was a remarkable sight. I'm glad you've joined our family.

Griffin looked puzzled by her statement but only said, "thank you."

Herman grabbed Griffin by the arm and introduced him to Odette's Grandpa and asked if the men wanted to join him in the den to watch NASCAR, so the ladies could cook and chat. Griffin didn't complain, he hugged Odette and followed the older gentlemen into another room.

While the ladies finished cooking, Odette's Grandma said to her, "you mother has explained very little to me about your relationship with Griffin, other than to tell me you are married and now pregnant. Are you happy?"

Odette answered, "I'm over the moon happy, Grandma. Griffin is a God-send."

"Speaking of God, is he a believer?" Her Grandma asked.

"Yes, he is," Odette informed.

Her Grandma said, "wonderful! Now I need to ask you something. May I have a few moments alone with him? I must ask him a few questions to ease my mind."

"I'm sure he'd love speaking with you. When?" Odette inquired.

Grandma looked out the kitchen window and replied, "send him outside with a glass of iced tea to give me. I'll be waiting for him in the swing your dad has by the lake."

Odette gave her Grandma a few minutes to get seated outside then she poured a glass of tea and went to get Griffin. "Griffin, will you do me a favor?" She asked.

"Sure, what?" He asked.

"Grandma went outside. Will you take her this glass of tea, so she doesn't get too hot? Mom said it will be a few more minutes before dinner is ready," she answered.

Griffin took the glass of tea and went outside to his new relative. When he came near, she said, "take a seat next to me, Griffin. I would like to chat."

He couldn't resist the elder version of Odette and sat next to her on the bench. He handed her the tea and commented, "this place is beautiful. I love the lake. The last time I was here I didn't notice it outside."

"Yes, it is lovely. I asked to meet you here, Griffin. Can I ask you a few questions?" Martha asked him.

Staring into her lovely green eyes, he said, "yes."

Martha continues, "has Odette told you about her heritage?"

"No, she hasn't. I was allowing everything to unfold on her terms. Is there something she needs to tell me?" He asked in return.

"I'm going to start at the beginning and say this, Odette doesn't know much. It's been a secret until recently. Charlene told me she's only known a few weeks. Odette is one quarter Creek Indian, Griffin," she explained.

Griffin was stunned and replies, "that is why you said I looked like Charlene's father. This explains a lot to me, I thought it strange when I first met Odette's mother and she had stared at me."

"They never knew him, Griffin. Would you like to know why?" She asked him.

He said, "if it's important."

Martha explained everything about how she and Chad met and fell in love, where they ran away too, and then stopped when she got to the place that plagued her soul for so many years, "when we found out I was pregnant with Charlene, we came out of hiding and called our parents. Within a few days, they managed to find us in Panama City.

Neither Chad's or my family were pleased, but Mr. Clearwater was adamant that we end the pregnancy and go our separate ways. We wanted no part of this demand on us and a family feud began, and my Chad was killed in an unnecessary scuffle.

What I need to know something from you and I want honesty. Do your parents approve of your marriage to my Granddaughter. I don't think I can live through another feud over racial issues," she exclaimed.

Griffin's heart was moved by Martha's frankness and he truthfully replied, "it's only Mom and me. My Dad died many years ago in an accident. Mom is against our marriage. She's only interested in the baby."

"Then I'm saying this to you, Griffin. Whether you see it or not, your mother is feuding with Odette. One day, it will backfire if you don't help them see eye-to-eye. Tell her what you know. If she's convinced that Odette is part Creek, then her heart will change. Don't waste time," she emphasized.

Griffin admits, "I won't have a problem with Odette, she wants peace. It may take a few tries to convince Mom. If I had evidence of Odette's heritage to show her, she may come around."

"Charlene has a few pictures of her father. We don't have anything else because I didn't marry him. Ask if you can borrow them and we will leave the rest to God," she states.

"Sounds good. I'll have Odette ask her and I'll pray about it too," Griffin said with a smile.

Martha patted him on the leg and said, "grant this old woman one more promise. Dedicate your baby to Jesus soon. I didn't have the chance to convert Chad to Christianity before he died, and Charlene didn't get her father's sacrificial blessing. I had to do it in his place. It's more important if two people do this."

Again, Griffin was puzzled by this lady's statement and he asked, "what do you mean by a sacrificial blessing? I can't promise something I don't understand."

"Why don't you read it for yourself from the Bible. It all began with Abraham and Isaac," she answered before rising from her seat and walking with Griffin back to the house.

"

Time To Wave the White Flag

Abba said to Jesus, "Martha is on top of this. She understands the importance of baby dedication and ending family feuds. Help Griffin find the way."

"He won't like traveling back to Oklahoma and facing his Mom, but I'm planning to show him another way that he can end this feud quickly. I also have a surprise that will heal a hurtful wound he still carries," Jesus said.

"Get on it, I'm ready for this to end so my little couple can build a new life and Zion can have a new addition to our spiritual family," Abba states.

Odette didn't question Griffin about Grandma's meeting with him until they were in her Jeep driving to her apartment. She said, "you and Grandma were extremely chummy before dinner. What did the two of you talk about at the lake?"

"Your heritage and the fact I may need to hold a peace treaty between you and Mom over our racial differences," he answered.

"She told you about Mom's real Dad?" Odette asked.

Griffin confesses, "I'm glad she did. She gave me an idea."

"What?" Odette inquired.

"Presenting Mom with evidence that you are part Creek Indian. Grandma said your mother has a few photographs of her father. If I showed them to her, she may come around. It's because you aren't Creek that Mom has troubles coming to terms with our marriage. Will you ask your mother if she will loan the pictures to us?" Griffin asked her.

They were at Odette's apartment when he asked, so we had an angel bring something else to Odette's memory. "Why don't we show her the pictures of Chad along with my artifacts? Zion said they were for my children. Your Mom doesn't have to know they were a recent find. It will prove to her that we love our heritage," she exclaims.

"That's a great idea. Show me your treasures," Griffin says.

Odette welcomed Griffin inside her small apartment and he instantly noticed how well she had her place decorated. He was impressed enough to say, "I can see why you said I lived like a homeless man. You have a lovely place. I can't wait to see how you'll decorate our home."

"I'm going to have fun, that's for sure. I love to decorate," she states.

Odette took him inside of the bedroom and dropped to her knees beside the bed. "What are you doing, Odette?" Griffin worriedly asked.

"I have the artifacts under my bed," she said.

Griffin looked closely at the bowl and pointed something out to Odette. On the bottom, and clearly visible after many years under water, was a Creek trademark that verified they had something to show his mother.

Griffin said, "I wish I could show Mom this without having to go back to Oklahoma."

"Did you ever see Lucy use Skype on your computer at the clinic?" Odette asked.

He said, "Yeah! She used it a lot to talk with pharmaceutical suppliers. It made it easier for us to order the medicine we had to have. What do you have in mind?"

Odette grinned at her husband and shared, "we can call Lucy and ask her to find a way to get your mother in front of a computer for a Skype call from us. That way, we can show her the pictures and the bowl. Easy peasy!:"

"Odette, you're amazing. I love the way you think. Can we do it tomorrow? If so, I'll call Lucy now, so she can get moving on her end," Griffin excitedly replied.

"We can do it tonight if Lucy can find your mother before long," Odette informed him.

"How, we don't have the pictures of your Grandfather yet?" He asked.

Odette picked up her phone and called her mother. When Charlene answered, Odette said, "hi, Mom. I know it's getting late, but will you take photograph the pictures you have of your Dad and send them to me as soon as possible. Griffin wants to prove to his mother that I'm part native American."

In moments, Odette had three pictures of Chad Clearwater on her phone and while she downloaded them to her computer for safekeeping, Griffin called Lucy. Next step was having someone find his Mom for a Skype call.

It was 9:00 p.m. in Georgia, but only 6:00 p.m. in Oklahoma when Lucy called Griffin back. "Griffin, Johnson has your mother and they are heading to my house. She should be here in a few minutes and I will Skype you then, just give me the access."

Griffin and Odette didn't have to wait long for Lucy to Skype to Odette's apartment computer. Griffin sat in a chair, so he could speak to his mother. As soon as her face came online, he said, "hi, Mom. It's good to see you. I love you."

"Son, seeing you on Lucy's computer is wonderful. Are you okay? When are you coming home?" She asked.

Griffin didn't answer her question, he immediately went into why he called, "I have something to tell you that may make your night. Remember how you objected to me marrying Odette because she was white? Well, I have news for you, she is part Creek Indian. We have pictures of her Grandfather to show you."

"Really, who are her relatives?" His mother asked.

Griffin held up a sheet of paper with the three photo's printed on them, so his mom could see them and said, Odette's mother is a Clearwater. Her Dad is Chad Clearwater."

"I know a few Clearwater people, Griffin. I wonder if they are related to her. I'll ask around," she said.

"Don't do that Mom. Chad was killed before he could marry Odette's Grandmother. It seems his family disapproved of her and it caused a family feud that didn't end well. Chad was killed in a family scuffle. It was her Grandmother that asked me to inform you, so you wouldn't disapprove of Odette any longer," Griffin informed her.

"It's said that Chad died. Her Grandmother is a wise woman. Knowing this has eased my heart. May I speak with her?" His mother asked.

Odette came to the computer and when she did, Irene, said, "Odette, can you forgive this old woman? I look forward to showing you more of our ways."

Odette, replied, "I'll be happy to forget your words to me. I want to show you something while we have you online."

Odette turns around and gets the bowl and brings it closer to the computer and turns it over for Irene to see the bottom and said, "Griffin wanted you to see my treasure. He said it has a Creek trademark on the bottom. Can you see it?"

"Yes, I can see it clearly. Do you have many relics?" Irene asked.

Odette answers, "no, but I plan to locate more someday."

Griffin returns to the computer ready to say the difficult things he had to say to his Mom, "I have something to say to you that may be difficult for you to hear. Don't say anything until I finish.

I've converted to Christianity and I've never been happier. We won't be returning to Oklahoma to live, but we plan to visit, Mom. Odette is pregnant, and we've decided to establish our own home in Florida."

Griffin braced himself for a verbal explosion and was shocked when his mother softly says to him with glistening eyes full of tears, "I've been visiting churches myself with your Uncle Randy and have a better understanding of the religion. He and I felt like you wouldn't be coming home to stay after leaving the way you did. Promise me, though, you'll come back often where I can see my grandchild grow."

Griffin was dumbfounded. He blurts out, "Randy and you have attended churches? What prompted that?

We want you to know your grandchildren and we want them to know their heritage. And if you want, I'll make sure you have a flight to visit anytime."

"I'm glad you want me in your life. I can't wait to see the baby. I'd like to be around when it makes an entrance into this world.

You wanted to know about Randy. Well, his time in jail after he set fire to your clinic sobered him up. He met a preacher while he was inside the jail that changed his heart. Since his release, he visits a non-denominational church in town and I've gone with him a few times. I may go more now that you've converted," she admits.

When they left the Skype call, Griffin was stunned enough to admit to Odette he had no clue our love extended that far. He said to her, "since I first laid eyes on Jesus, my life has turned around, He has been working overtime for me and my family. I'd given up hope of anything or anybody helping Randy sober himself. We all tried for years and failed. Now, Mom wants to know more about Christianity. It's a miracle."

After saying that, Griffin took the artifact back to the bedroom and stowed it under the bed until they packed. When he raised up he saw another Bible on a nightstand. Then he remembered the other thing Odette's Grandmother requested.

The Final Stage Gets Set

Griffin picks up the Bible and asks, "how many of these books do you own, Odette?"

Odette laughed, "I been given quite a few over the years, but the one I have in the condominium is my favorite."

"Why?" Griffin inquired.

"It's written in layman's terms without the religious phrases," she answered.

"Your Grandma asks me to promise her something else. I said I couldn't because I didn't understand what she meant, and she said I needed to read the story about Abraham and Isaac from the Bible," he shared.

"That's interesting. What specifically did she ask you to do?" Odette asks.

Griffin hesitated a moment and said, "she wants me to dedicate our baby to God soon as a sacrificial blessing. Do you understand this request?

"I think I do, I've seen couples do this in church with their newborns. I think it means they want the child raised in Christianity. Read what Grandma said and pray about it. If you don't understand ask Jesus to clarify things for you. Remember when I said He cleared-up a lot of scriptures for me that I didn't understand properly?" Odette recommended.

That night while Odette slept, Griffin read the story of Abraham and Isaac in the book of Genesis. The story left him with many unexplained questions. The only thing he gathered from the written passages was that Isaac was spared, but he didn't know why from the verses he read.

Later that night when Griffin was asleep, he was given a dream of a baby being killed. The dream looped over and over until it became a nightmare and had him twisting and turning in bed. When he awakened from the torturing sleep, he didn't have the opportunity to ask Jesus for help because they were disturbed by a knock on Odette's apartment door.

Herman, Odette's Dad was standing in the doorway when they looked outside. When Griffin opened the door, Herman said while pointing to his car, "Charlene and I were hoping the two of you were awake. We have some boxes for you to pack Odette's things. We should have given them to you last night, but we forgot and since we were headed this way to Sunday School, we thought we'd bring them to you."

The couple gathered the boxes from the back of Herman's truck and brought them inside and started packing after a quick breakfast which kept Griffin's mind on other things. They worked steadily throughout the day and were both too tired to talk much at dinner, but when Griffin fell asleep the same disturbing dream returned.

For three more days, Griffin refused to call on Jesus about a nightmare. He felt it would hinder them if he spent time sorting through the reason he kept having the dream. Instead, he and Odette stayed busy taking care of legalities, and other details, so they could finish everything before moving into their new home.

It was Tuesday evening, the second night they were in Albany, right after Odette arranged for her things to be picked-up by a storage facility, that she noticed Griffin wasn't acting right. "What's wrong, Griffin? You seem distracted and you don't look well," she asked.

He answered, "I'm tired. I haven't been sleeping well."

"It's probably my bed. It's too small for us and the mattress is old. I plan to put the bedroom set in another room when we move and buy us a new set. One big enough for us to maneuver around on," she said with a wink.

Instead of saying anything to her about the recurring dream, he agreed with her that it was probably the small bed since the dreams started the first night he slept on that bed. That night the same angel that was assigned to give Griffin the dream took drastic measures and increased Griffin's torment. He appeared in Griffin's dream and demanded he turns his back on his family. Griffin refuses in his dream and the cruel messenger kept tormenting him and said they had to die. He even showed Griffin that Jesus was behind the request.

Griffin woke from his dream crying. He couldn't believe the sweet Jesus he knew would want him to abandon his precious family, and if he didn't they had to die. He gathered strength enough to go in the kitchen where he made a cup of coffee, so he wouldn't go back to sleep. Then picked up the Bible and cried out to Jesus for answers.

"Lord, since I read the story about Abraham and Isaac, I've had nightmares every night. Tonight, was worse. Can you explain why you would want me to abandon my family? I can't do that," Griffin cries.

Jesus appears to him and answers his question, "I'm glad you want me to interpret the scriptures for you. When God told Abraham to kill his son, He did mean literally. God wanted Abraham to sever ties with the boy and give his life over to Him for well keeping. In Abraham's day, people sacrificed children on alters but God wanted to show Abraham what He truly wanted.

The apostle Paul explains this better in the book of Romans. You see, Abraham dealt with killing Isaac buy convincing himself that God could recreate his son. God had given Isaac to him and Sarah when they were too old to have children, so he trusted God to do it again because of what God said about Isaac before he was born.

The miracle wasn't in what God could do for Abraham, but in what Abraham entered into by trusting God. After a mental struggle that almost killed them both, God sent a replacement for the physical offering that set the stage for me to come into the world much later.

I don't want you to abandon your family. What I would like is to have you give them to me for safekeeping. Release your hold to guide, support, and provide for them like God does for me. I need to have leadership in your family for you, Odette, and the baby to feel safe and secure in God's love."

"I admitted to Odette a few hours ago that I've never been happier since meeting you. I understand what you mean, but how does this work," Griffin asked.

Jesus reminds Griffin, "do you remember Zion telling you that the burden to take care of your mother's problems was too heavy for you to bear?"

"Yes," Griffin replied.

Countering Jesus says, "without a spiritual leader watching over every detail, obstacles in life make people struggle unnecessarily. That's why I say to cast your cares on me. I'm the only person who has spiritual authority over life, no other man has it because God made me King of all life.

I'm the Judge, only my say so matters to the angels who watch over you. When you come to me for help, life gets easier, problems are solved or made easier to cope with until strength to overcome them arise. Don't you want to be free of the burden? Hasn't your life been easier since Zion told you not to fret over your mother?

Give your responsibility for Odette and the baby over to me so you and them can live in grace, peace, and mercy inside of God's love. We want you to rest in God's kingdom on earth. In the heart of Zion, your hearts with change, and she can help you see your true desires. All we desire is love."

Griffin nodded but did say anything else. He needed time to mull over what he'd just learned. Instead, he cleaned up the mess and repacked the coffee pot and cup and went to wake Odette.

He didn't say anything to her and after they dressed, they packed the suitcase in the jeep and drove to her parent's house for a quick breakfast. It took a few hours before they could leave. The Paynes had things to say and give to them before they left. Then they had to go over details with Odette's Dad, so he would know what to do about her things before the first of the month.

Odette hugs her Dad and gives him the apartment key then she turns to her mother and hugs and kisses her to say goodbye, Griffin waves still uncomfortable with kissing them. It was almost 4:00 p.m. before they left Albany to return to the condominium in Panama City.

Griffin didn't talk at all during their trip back. Odette was exhausted and fell asleep while he drove, but as soon as they arrived back at the condominium, Griffin took a few things upstairs for Odette and then took her hand before she had a chance to get comfortable, "follow me to the beach, Odette."

"Okay, is there a reason you want a walk on the beach this late in the day?" She asked.

He said, "I'll tell you when we are at water's edge"

When their bare feet touched the water, Griffin turned Odette to face him and said, "remember when we lie in bed back in Oklahoma and you introduced me to Jesus? Zion was also there with us and that's when my life started to change for the better.

I've asked them to meet us here on the beach. I have something I must do before the sun goes down, and I'd like it to be in a place we both love," Griffin told her.

Odette understood Griffin was very emotional, so she didn't say a word only shook her head in agreement. When he had her agreement, he spoke softly into the wind, "Jesus, will you and Zion please join us. I'm ready to do what you want."

Not only did Jesus come into their spiritual sight, Zion and Abba did as well. I stood in the backdrop ready to show my approval when the dead was done.

Griffin fell to his knees, wrapped his arms around her legs and placed his head on Odette's pregnant belly, then in his native tongue, he prayerfully gave their baby's spirit to Jesus before it was even born.

Odette looked at him confused and he said, "Jesus has our baby's spirit. We are not strong enough to provide what he needs to live a prosperous and healthy life. I Jesus to watch over our treasure."

Griffin stood and took Odette by the chin, and looked deep into her eyes and said, "Jesus, I want you to be Odette's spiritual husband, I'm comfortable being her best friend and soulmate.

I promise from this moment on, I will allow you to guide and take care of her and I will enjoy my life by her side. When she faces problems, we will come to you together with the issues. I will trust you to see us through. I have learned from experience how hard life is and I don't wish that on my family. Thank you for wanting the complete say over this family."

When Griffin finished talking, Jesus said, "it's my turn to show you what's in my heart."

Griffin and Odette both turned in His direction to see what He wanted. They watched Jesus take the tiny spirit of their unborn baby and give it to His Father. God kissed the tiny seed and handed it over to its true mother.

When Zion, (creation itself) held the baby's spirit in her grasp she began to cry joyous tears. Then she started singing the songs Abba loved to hear her sing to the new little spirit. Then she walked up to Odette and place her hands inside Odette's womb returning the spiritual seed back to the baby's tiny body.

Seeing Abba's mission completed and His heart full overtook me and with Zion's help, I transformed myself into three creatures, so I could celebrate and impress Griffin and Odette in a manner they would appreciate.

I jumped in the sea as a dolphin, I howled at the moon as a wolf, and I whooped like the swan back in Oklahoma. I was overjoyed that Griffin's and Odette's new life was now in our care. With our help, they were free to love and enjoy their lives the way God planned. Most of all, we would get to hear Zion sing for many generations as I told this story to millions.

Prologue

From the beginning of time, God only wanted a family to love and enjoy. He wanted to watch them grow and thrive under Zion's influence and wisdom.

Romans 8:19-30: New International Version Bible

[19] For the creation waits in eager expectation for the children of God to be revealed. [20] For the creation was subjected to frustration, not by its own choice, but by the will of the one who subjected it, in hope 21 that the creation itself will be liberated from its bondage to decay and brought into the freedom and glory of the children of God.

[22] We know that the whole creation has been groaning as in the pains of childbirth right up to the present time. [23] Not only so, but we ourselves, who have the firstfruits of the Spirit, groan inwardly as we wait eagerly for our adoption to sonship, the redemption of our bodies. [24] For in this hope we were saved. But hope that is seen is no hope at all. Who hopes for what they already have? [25] But if we hope for what we do not yet have, we wait for it patiently.

[26] In the same way, the Spirit helps us in our weakness. We do not know what we ought to pray for, but the Spirit himself intercedes for us through wordless groans. [27] And he who searches our hearts knows the mind of the Spirit because the Spirit intercedes for God's people in accordance with the will of God.

[28] And we know that in all things God works for the good of those who love him, who have been called according to his purpose. [29] For those God foreknew he also predestined to be conformed to the image of his Son, that he might be the firstborn among many brothers and sisters. [30] And those he predestined, he also called; those he called, he also justified; those he justified, he also glorified.

Bibliography
Galatians 5:22 New American Standard
Galatians 5:22 Message Bible
Romans 8:19-30 New International Version

About the Author

Raven H. Price is a Christian fiction writer who uses romance mixed with fantasy and supernatural events to intrigue her readers. She also enjoys devoting her time to inspiring and encouraging people to believe in themselves and trusting in a loving God.

She is happily married to her husband, Ralph W. Price, III, and they live in Leesburg, Georgia with four cats. Since she is a cat lover, her Twitter handle is 'roaringpurr.' Her Facebook author page @Roaringpurr is devoted not only to her books but as an outlet to encourage love, respect, and acceptance of all humanity.

Please consider leaving a review on Amazon by clicking on this, thank you.

www.ingramcontent.com/pod-product-compliance
Lightning Source LLC
Chambersburg PA
CBHW070324260626
47160CB00003B/947